Spencer stepped forward, erasing the small space between them.

His thumbs ran along Tatum's jawline, tracing the soft skin of her neck and the shell of her ear. She closed her eyes and her lips parted, her breath escaping on unsteady gasps. He watched her response, her arousal driving him crazy. "How long?" he asked, his tone soft.

Her green eyes fluttered open. "How long?" she repeated, breathless.

"Since you've been...kissed." He bit out the last word. "How long has it been since a man's loved your body?"

"My body is none of your business." But the tremor in her voice told him he wasn't imagining this. Her hands gripped the counter edge as if she was holding herself back. She wanted him, even if she didn't want to accept it.

"And it's a damn shame," he murmured, longing to pry her hands from the counter, to feel her fingers slide through his hair. Before he was through, she'd be holding on to him...

D1011862

Dear Reader,

There's nothing like your first love. It's intense and fiery, sweet and all-consuming—if it ends, the pain can be equally so. It took years for Tatum and Spencer to get over the wounds their long-ago breakup caused. But now that they're thrown together again, their wounds take a backseat to the power of their attraction. Tatum's never wanted someone like she wants Spencer. And Spencer's never wanted anyone but Tatum. Once they give in to one another, neither is prepared for how severely their worlds are rocked.

Between the Christmas caroling, wedding showers and bedroom adventures, Spencer does his best to wear down Tatum's resistance. But no matter how willing Tatum is to have Spencer in her bed, her heart is off-limits. Her heart is too broken to try love again.

I adore first-love stories. There's something raw and vulnerable about them. And Tatum and Spencer are about as raw as a couple can get. Helping them make their way back to each other, find forgiveness and trust, is quite the emotional roller coaster—let me tell you. But I hope you enjoy the ride as much as I did!

I love to hear from readers so please find me on my website, sashasummers.com, on Facebook or Twitter, @sashawrites.

Enjoy every page,

Sasha Summers

Sasha Summers

—

Christmas in His Bed

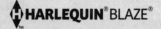

⟨H⟩ HARLEQUIN® BLAZE®

Recycling programs
for this product may
not exist in your area.

ISBN-13: 978-0-373-79922-0

Christmas in His Bed

Copyright © 2016 by Sasha Best

Printed in U.S.A.

www.Harlequin.com

Sasha Summers grew up surrounded by books. Her passions have always been storytelling, romance and travel. Whether it's an easy-on-the-eyes cowboy or a hero of truly mythic proportions, Sasha falls a little in love with each and every one of her heroes. She frequently gets lost with her characters in the worlds she creates, forgetting those everyday tasks like laundry and dishes. Luckily, her four brilliant children and hero-inspiring hubby are super understanding and helpful.

Books by Sasha Summers

Harlequin American Romance

The Boones of Texas

A Cowboy's Christmas Reunion
Twins for the Rebel Cowboy
Courted by the Cowboy

Harlequin Blaze

Seducing the Best Man

To get the inside scoop on Harlequin Blaze and its talented writers, visit Facebook.com/BlazeAuthors.

All backlist available in ebook format.

Visit the Author Profile page at Harlequin.com for more titles.

Acknowledgments

Thank you to my amazing writer peeps. Writing might be a solitary profession, but I never feel alone. Your support and belief keep me writing.

Thanks, always, to my wonderful agent, Pamela Hopkins, and awesome editor, Johanna Raisanen. Your faith in my books means the world!

And my family—you guys are the best. I love you.

Dedication
To those whose first love is still their only love.

1

BEING BRALESS WAS as close to rebellious as Tatum had been in almost a decade. So was reading her third romance novel in a row, barely emerging from the nest of quilts she'd dragged to the comfy rocking chair in front of the now-dying fire. No makeup, no expectations, no worries. Day one of her new life was good.

When she was done reading, she could dig through her suitcase for her vibrator and some quality alone time. Or she could stay up reading all night long.

For the first time in her life, there was no one to stop her from doing whatever she wanted. And knowing that was...*awesome*.

She glanced at the old cuckoo clock over the mantel. Right now her ex-husband, Brent, and the new Mrs. Cahill, Kendra, were probably sipping umbrella drinks on some beach somewhere—if he'd actually taken a vacation. But knowing Kendra, she wouldn't have given him a choice.

She burrowed into her quilts and added the book she'd finished to the pile at her feet. Her evening would be far more satisfying than a night with Brent and his tiny penis. Penis size aside, he had no stamina and had never taken an active interest in giving her pleasure. Tatum had always waited for him to head to the shower before finishing things off right with her handy-dandy purple-swirly love machine. She called him Chris, after her favorite movie actor. Brent and Chris had never met. Brent had no idea Chris existed.

She drained hot chocolate from her large Santa mug and stood, padding across the wooden floor in her socks and slippers to restart the Nat King Cole album. Maybe it was wrong that she was in such a good mood, newly divorced and absolutely alone on Christmas. But she was. She wanted to be happy. And right now, Nat King Cole, stimulating romance novels and copious amounts of hot chocolate were all she needed to be happy. And, maybe later, Chris.

She picked up the last book on the side table, reading the back blurb and its tantalizing promise of "eroticism on every page" with a sigh. But a slight movement from out the large picture window caught her eye. She froze, a prick of fear running down her spine.

A man stood on her front porch railing. A big man. So tall she couldn't see his head or shoulders as he reached for something on the roof.

She edged closer to the fireplace and the brass poker resting against the wall. She might be alone, but she wasn't helpless. She gripped the poker and made her way closer to the window.

But the man wasn't armed with a weapon. He had a large coil of Christmas lights hanging around his shoulder. Christmas lights. She didn't drop the poker, but her swing-first-question-second instinct wavered. Something about a man hanging Christmas lights brought the threat level down.

She lowered her weapon, watching as the man moved along the porch railing with ease, threading the heavy strand of lights on unseen hooks. He was fast. But why was he there, working so hard to decorate her house? He must run one of those decorating services. Maybe he was at the wrong house? She should stop him before he got too far.

She wrapped a throw around her shoulders and pushed through the front door, still holding her poker. A blast of cold air cut through her sweats and the thermal underwear beneath. *Shit, shit and double shit.* She'd forgotten how frigid North Texas could get. She hurried across the porch, but stopped a few feet from the man on the railing.

His leather jacket rode up as he worked. And his stomach… She swallowed. *What a view.* He stretched, exposing more actual man flesh than she'd seen in oh so long. And it was amazing. The kind of amazing even the best romance novels would have a hard time capturing.

Cut. Hard. All man. Every cleft and ridge of his six-pack was on display. His jeans hung low enough to reveal the edge of his hips. Just looking at him made her light-headed. Stunned. Excited. Achy.

Something deep inside her turned molten and fluid.

Her fingers twisted in the throw around her shoulders as her gaze followed the impressively dark happy trail that disappeared beneath the waistband of his jeans. What sort of surprises would be found underneath the skintight, faded jeans that clung to this man's hips? She swallowed, her imagination offering up all sorts of possibilities. She was oh so tempted to touch that stomach.

Which was wrong. And completely unexpected. She'd never *ever* do something so irrational but…

But all that muscle and strength, the dark lines of a

tattoo peeking wickedly from under the edge of his shirt, had her utterly captivated. What would it be like to touch a man like *this*? Better yet, what would it be like to have *him* touch *her*? A shiver racked her body. Brent had very specific preferences in bed—namely her lying still beneath him, quiet, aching for something more. Wanting something…more. *More…like this.*

She pressed her hand against her stomach and the delicious flare of liquid heat that coiled inside her. Maybe all that reading was getting to her.

This man wasn't supposed to be here; he might even get in trouble for being here if he was hired to holiday-fy another house. She stepped closer, surprised to hear him humming a Christmas carol. The sound was deep and rough, an undeniable turn-on.

"Excuse me?" she said. "I think there's been a mistake."

No response. But one arm went higher, revealing more of the tattoo on his side. A feather? A quill? Covering a long scar along his ribs… And more muscles.

"Hello?" she tried again, a little louder.

He was on one foot then, reaching for something on the roof.

She stepped forward, considering the best way to get his attention. She blew out a deep breath. This was ridiculous. What was the matter with her? She reached out and tugged on one of his jeans belt loops.

"Hold up," he called out. "Almost…got…it." The strand of Christmas lights came on, casting the porch in hues of red and green.

She held her breath as he leaped down, eager to see what the rest of this man looked like. But the clear blue eyes that greeted her were a total surprise. The kind of surprise that left her breathless—and shocked.

No.

"Spencer?" Her voice was high and tight. Even now, after years, she knew him. Instant recognition—instant reaction. Her heart twisted sharply at the all-too-familiar blue eyes regarding her in astonishment. And her body was racked with something he'd inspired whenever he was close to her: desire.

Spencer Ryan. The very last person she wanted to see right now.

He stared at her, frozen. Why was he acting so surprised? It was her house. A house she'd practically run from years ago, because of him. *She* had every right to be here. *He* did not. She welcomed the anger warming her belly. Anger was good. Much better than…the other feelings bouncing around inside of her.

His gaze sharpened, searching hers. She tried to ignore that familiar pull tightening the pit of her stomach. "Tatum?" His voice was low, husky.

"Yeah… Hi," she croaked. *This is bad.* So, *so* bad. Like she needed another bump to her already dinged confidence. Nothing like coming face-to-face with the man who had humiliated her, destroying her heart and her fragile ego eight years before. Yes, it was the holidays and there'd been a *chance* she'd run into him. But she'd hoped she wouldn't. Definitely not her first night home. Not when she wasn't ready to face him. And certainly not with crazy hair and no bra.

She tore her gaze from his, wrapping her arms around her waist. All the muscle and sexiness was Spencer? What the hell had happened to him? *This* Spencer barely resembled the clean-cut boy she'd held hands with in the halls of Greyson High School. Now he was big, almost intimidating—with shaggy black hair, a thick stubble covering his angular jaw and a new wariness about his clear blue eyes. Those eyes.

She forced her gaze away. She would not think about his eyes. Or his body. Or those abs. And that tattoo… Her pulse was racing just standing there. He was all hot in his gloriously ass-hugging jeans and broad-shoulder-hugging jacket while she wore a blanket.

"It's been a long time," he said, finally smiling. He hesitated briefly before pulling her against him in a warm embrace.

She stiffened. She didn't want to hug him. He might look good—who was she kidding, he looked frigging amazing—but she knew what he was capable of. What sort of pain he could inflict. She knew that but… His hand pressed, open, against the base of her back. Even through the layers of fabric, she could feel the contours of his fingers and the warmth of his palm. And it—he—felt good.

Then she took a deep breath and inhaled his scent. She swallowed, trembling. Dammit. He smelled the same, teasing her…flooding every cell with a steady throb of want. "It has." She didn't know where the overwhelming urge to hold on to him came from, but she fought it. It shouldn't matter that it had been too long since anyone had held her close. She wasn't going to melt in *his* arms.

She pushed away from him, stepping back quickly.

His smile faded as he eyed the poker in her hands. "Prepared for battle?"

She blinked, looking at him, then the poker. "What?"

"Or is it some new fashion accessory I don't know about?" He shot another pointed glance at the poker, crossing his thick arms over his broad chest. If she wasn't pissed as hell at his sudden and irritating reappearance in her life, she might admire the shift of muscle in his forearms. But she was. She was pissed.

"Where I come from, a woman alone protects herself from strange men hanging off their porches." She sounded unruffled and together—revealing none of her inner turmoil. "Especially when it's in the middle of the night."

He glanced at the open door behind her, then back at her.

"I'm a little tired for company and, since it is late, it's best if you go," she said over her shoulder, heading back inside and out of the cold—away from him. Her voice wasn't shaking. She didn't look like she was retreating. Even if that was sort of what she was doing. But she sort of had to because she couldn't seem to get a handle on the way she was reacting to him.

But he didn't move. He just stood there, a strange expression on his face. "I'm sorry I scared you." He held up his hands. "If I'd known you were here, alone, I would have said something first."

"Before you decorated my house?" she asked, holding the doorknob.

He planted his hands on his hips and shook his head. "Yeah, about that. It was made perfectly clear by the lady in charge that this needed to be done now or suffer the consequences."

What the hell did that mean? "The lady in charge? Sounds like your wife takes the holidays as seriously as your mother."

"*No* wife," he clarified, placing an odd emphasis on the word *no* before chuckling. "I was talking about the head of the neighborhood association."

"Why would they bother you with that?" she asked, more and more confused.

He pulled his keys from his pocket, watching her intently. "Guess Brent didn't tell you I was renting the place?"

Her lungs emptied painfully. "No, no, he didn't," she muttered, reeling. Brent hadn't told her a lot of things.

"Six months now. After the last tenants left? You didn't notice my stuff? In the master bedroom?"

"I didn't know," she murmured. "I'm staying in my old room." Was this Brent's idea of a joke? Not that she'd told him much about Spencer. But he knew enough. He knew Spencer Ryan had been her first love and that he'd broken her heart.

And now he was living in her house. The place she needed to regroup and recover.

"You remember how the town gets around the holidays?" he asked, seemingly unaware of her discomfort. "That hasn't changed." He shrugged. "I've been on assignment for over a week and I'm running out of time. So that's why I was hanging lights. Now. At night. In the cold."

He was decorating her house…because it was also his house? It wasn't some horrible mistake. But what the hell was she supposed to do? It wasn't like she was going to let him stay. No matter what time of the night it was. But she couldn't think of a single coherent thing to say.

He shivered. "It's a damn cold night." He grinned.

"I guess this means I have to let you in?" she asked, seriously considering shutting the door in his grinning face. He thought this was funny? Did he not remember the last time they saw each other? The things he'd said? She thought she'd never recover.

"That'd be the neighborly thing to do." He brushed past her, elbowing the door shut behind him.

"Right. Neighborly," she tried not to snap. Why was he surveying the room?

Why did he have to have that ass?

Her anger died a little. It was really hard to hate him while thoroughly appreciating the way his jeans hugged the muscles of his thighs. And his ass. That was definitely worth a long, thorough inspection. She swallowed, forcing her eyes up before he saw her. But he was still looking around the house, curious. "What are you looking for?"

He turned, his blue gaze pinning hers, and shook his head. "Nothing."

Obviously he was lying. It was clear he was looking for something. But what. His gaze was far too…intense and probing. And more than a little unsettling. More than a little…affecting. But words wouldn't come.

"Home for the holidays?" he asked, his voice deep and rough.

She mumbled, "Yes." Then added, "And no." Why was she answering him? Why wasn't she telling him to leave?

His crooked grin caused her heart to thump heavily in her chest. Not the most reassuring response. "That's cryptic." He shook his head.

Maybe it was, but she didn't feel the need to say more. Yet she couldn't seem to manage, "Get out now," so she stood there, her awareness increasing and the silence stretching out. He sighed, that gaze never leaving her face. She couldn't seem to look away. Or think. A cold shower was definitely in her future. Or Chris. Lots of Chris time.

He was saying something, but her mind was too busy processing *everything* to hear him. Oh, God. In less than thirty minutes she'd gone from content to distressed. And it was all Spencer's fault. Again.

"I'd offer to stay across the street at my mom's but she's got a full house, with the holidays and all." His words were soft, echoing in her ears.

She frowned at him, wrapping her arms around her waist. "One of us needs to find a hotel."

"I haven't slept in a few days, Tatum. I'd appreciate one night in my own bed. I'm not here much—the empty fridge and pantry can confirm that. I'll stay out of your way." He did look tired. His blue eyes were bloodshot and there were bags under his eyes. "I don't even snore."

"Spencer—"

"I can move into your room," he offered.

He was sleeping in her parents' room. Which was good—she wasn't ready to go there. Any and all memories of her mom could wait behind that closed door for a few more days. "No," she said. "I w-wouldn't sleep in there."

"I'm sorry about your mom," he said, grabbing her attention.

Tatum nodded. She hadn't visited Greyson since her mother's death three years before. "It's strange to be here and have it so quiet." She shrugged, not wanting to share with him.

But Spencer had known better than most about her mother and her fits of temper. When she'd been on a real tear, her mother could be heard all up and down Maple Drive. Her mother's anger and bitterness had been one of the reasons she'd gone to live with her father her senior year of high school. Spencer had been the other.

"You look good, Tatum." His voice pitched low, all gravel.

She was acutely aware of the way his eyes leisurely swept her from head to toe. When his attention returned to her face, his jaw was locked. Was that disapproval on his face? Or—her heart was thumping—was it something else? She didn't know how to read the tension that rolled off of him. But it was unnerving as hell. His gaze narrowed, piercing hers. What was he trying to figure out?

"Tatum?" Her name. His voice. She felt a shudder run down her back.

"No, I don't." Her words spilled from her lips. She looked like hell and she knew it. "*You* look different," she admitted. *Different* was an understatement. Even if her response to him was the same: hyperaware. When he was close, she'd *felt* it. Right now, she was feeling all sorts of things that made her nervous and excited and tense. *Dammit.*

He cocked a questioning eyebrow her way.

She shrugged. "There's…more of you." Including abs and tattoos and the lovely dark happy trail disappearing beneath his waistband. She needed to stop talking—and thinking—immediately. Instead, she stared at his chest, encased in a skintight gray shirt and leather jacket. What was absolutely terrifying was how badly her fingers itched to explore him. *No. No exploring. Evicting. Immediate evicting.*

He laughed. "More of me?"

His laughter rolled over her, leaving her tingling in all the right places. *Dammit.* It was cruel that he'd turned out even more beautiful than she remembered. And completely unfair. He'd broken her heart, made her doubt her judgment and left her unbelieving she was worthy of love.

How dare he stand there, teasing her, acting like he wasn't the bad guy. She knew better. It wasn't like he was just some dangerously good-looking man making her house all festive while waking up every one of her lady-part nerves. If only that were the case.

"Tatum?" he whispered, coming to stand in front of her. "You okay?"

She nodded. Her attention wandered to his mouth, leaving her breathless. Would his touch feel the same? His lips had branded her skin, magic against her lips... No, she wasn't okay. If she was, she wouldn't be dragging up memories better left buried.

Besides, he didn't deserve to touch her. To kiss her. And she needed to stop thinking of that. Of him—naked. Of what she wanted to do to him—naked. This was Spencer. And the two of them would not be getting naked together.

Even if he is way more exciting than my vibrator. The thought sent another shudder through her.

"You cold?" His voice was gruff and rumbling—shaking her to the core.

"No," she managed, her tongue thick and her throat tight. She wasn't cold. For the first time in a long time, she was feeling delectably hot. The only problem with this scenario was *he* was the one making her feel this way.

She stepped around him, hoping to quiet the desire surging through her veins. Her overstimulated reaction to him made no sense. She didn't like him. *Maybe this is what happens when you go for more than a year without sex?* "But I need something to drink and you need to... to go to bed," she said, glancing at him. "One night," she added, knowing she was a coward. But it was after midnight, cold, and she wasn't heartless.

"Okay. One night. I'll crash here tonight and look into

staying somewhere else while you're in town." He was staring at her again. "If you're sure Brent won't mind?"

She nodded. *Brent so won't mind.* She headed into the kitchen, deliberately avoiding his gaze. She could sleep under the same roof; she could be an adult. But she wasn't going to talk about her marriage or her divorce with him.

He followed her. "Why is it so cold in here? Pilot light go out again?" he asked, rubbing his hands together. "Brent couldn't get it to work?"

"The heat won't come on." She pointed at the fireplace over her shoulder. "But at least I got the fire going, even if I did burn my thumb and singe some hair." She held her thumb up.

She hadn't expected him to cradle her hand in his or hold up her thumb for a thorough inspection. She wanted to yank her hand away and scowl at him… No, she didn't. Which was worse.

His gaze locked with hers. "Some homecoming." His hold went from reassuring to overwhelming. "I am sorry about tonight. Not the way I'd imagined seeing you again." His words shook her. The rhythmic stroke of his thumb along her wrist turned her insides fluid.

Not the way I'd imagined seeing you again.

She blew out a deep breath. "It's…it's fine." Her words were a raspy whisper but she managed to pull her hand from his. No touching. Touching was bad. And more space was good too. She stepped back, wrapping her arms around her waist. "I…I can call a repairman in the morning."

He glanced at her hand, then back at her, his eyes narrowing. "I'll fix it before we go to bed."

We go to bed. She swallowed, staring at the floor so her face wouldn't betray her thoughts. "Thanks."

"What's going on?" he asked softly.

"What do you mean?" She knew what he meant. But her life was none of his business. And, dammit, she was having a hard time thinking straight with him standing there staring at her that way. She needed to stay cool. And keep him at arm's length. So she busied herself in the kitchen, pulling out the milk, a saucepan and some cocoa packets.

He followed her, standing too close. "You're here alone, basically in the dark, without heat. Alone."

She put the kettle on the burner, her hands and her voice unsteady. "Did you have to say that twice?" she asked.

"I guess that's the thing I'm most hung up on," he confessed.

He was standing behind her, his warmth rolling over her. "It is?" She glanced back at him, the questions in his gaze enough to turn her back to cocoa making. "I assure you, you don't need to be hung up on *anything* that has to do with me, okay?" She tried to sound flippant but it didn't work.

"Old habits die hard. I know how to read you. I always have." There was an edge to his voice.

"Maybe. When we were kids," she agreed. But they definitely weren't kids anymore. And even if he had known what she was thinking—wanting—before she had, didn't mean he did now. That was a long time ago. "Right now I want cocoa. And peace and quiet." She spun around to face him, shoving the mug into his hand. "Good night."

"Trying to get rid of me?" he asked, glancing at the mug she'd placed in his hands before leveling her with the weight of his gaze once more.

"I didn't realize that was unclear."

He chuckled.

She was very proud that she didn't smile at him. Because his smile was hard to resist. He was hard to resist. Because, honestly, she would happily replace her swirly purple battery-operated love machine with this new manlier version of Spencer. She choked on her sip of cocoa. *Please, God, don't let him figure out what I'm thinking. And wanting.*

"Brent's not here." He paused. "You're alone." He swallowed, his gaze searching her face as he leaned forward, placing his mug on the counter, his large hands on either side of her—effectively pinning her against the counter.

"So?" She didn't deny it. She was alone. She was relieved her out-of-control hunger for him had somehow escaped his notice. But now that she was so close, that wouldn't last for long. Her heart was slamming against her ribs and breathing was becoming increasingly difficult. Because breathing drew in his scent, his tantalizing, captivating, enticing scent.

"And there's this." He pointed at her, then himself—stepping so close that his breath fanned her hair. "There's still a hell of a…connection between the two of us." He practically growled the words. Her body tightened, expectant, at the sound of his undeniable hunger.

For her.

His attention wandered to her mouth, leaving no doubt what he wanted. He felt it too. Of course he did.

She could sway into him, give in… But she should fight it. Even if his lips were so close. "Yes." It took a lot of effort to form a coherent answer.

"Yes?" he repeated, his nostrils flaring as his gaze locked with hers.

"Yes. I am alone." Her voice wavered.

He shook his head, the muscle in his jaw hard as rock. "That's all?" he asked. "I won't touch another man's wife." He ground out the words. "But, dammit, I want to kiss you so bad it hurts."

Kiss me. She stared at him, gripped by a crushing, desperate ache. *Touch me.* "I'm no man's wife. But I don't want you to kiss me," she whispered.

2

SPENCER STARED DOWN at her, his nerves strung so tight he worried he'd pop.

Tatum was here.

And all he could think about was touching her, tasting her. Silk. Warmth. Pure temptation. And even though he had no right to touch her, to think of her tangled up with him, he couldn't stop himself. His body responded to her without reason, as if they hadn't been living separate lives for years.

Her quiver revealed her lie. She wasn't immune to him.

"I don't believe you," he argued.

She drew in a wavering breath. "I don't care what you believe." There was an edge to her voice. She wasn't immune to him—but she was going to fight it.

Her green eyes clashed with his and he smiled at her. This was Tatum. The girl who'd stolen his heart, the girl he'd lived for. The girl he'd crushed, shredding his own heart in the process. He'd missed her every day for the last eight years.

He reached up, smoothing an errant curl from her forehead. "Your hair is longer."

She didn't say anything as he threaded the curl between his fingers. The curl coiled around him, clinging to him the way he envisioned her clinging to him.

"So is yours," she whispered.

A woman alone protects herself. He'd heard her. *No man's wife.* For the first time, nothing was stopping them. Except maybe the defiance in her gaze.

He saw the way she looked at his mouth, the way her lips parted and her hands tightened on the counter's edge. There was a restlessness about her he'd never seen in her before. She was nervous… That was obvious. Hell, he was nervous. But it was more than that. It was their past. What he'd done was reprehensible. Could she still hate him so much that she couldn't bear to be close to him?

Or did she hate that she still wanted him?

From the look on her face, it'd be all too easy to assume it was the latter. Because that was what he wanted. Badly. The way she was looking at him now, flushed and dazed, focused on his mouth… He hadn't been this hard since he was sixteen.

He stepped forward, erasing the small space between them. His thumbs ran along her jawline, tracing the soft skin of her neck and the shell of her ear. She closed her eyes, her lips parted, her breath escaping on unsteady gasps. He watched her response, her arousal driving him crazy. "How long?" he asked, his tone soft.

Her green eyes fluttered open. "How long?" she repeated, breathless.

"Since you've been…kissed." He bit out the last word. "How long has it been since a man's loved your body?"

"My body is none of your business." But the tremor in

her voice told him he wasn't imagining this. Her hands gripped the counter edge as if she was holding herself back. She wanted him, even if she didn't want to accept it.

"And it's a damn shame," he murmured, longing to pry her hands from the counter, to feel her fingers slide through his hair. Before he was through, she'd be holding on to him.

He smiled as his lips brushed her startled mouth— featherlight, a whisper of a touch. She shuddered as his nose traced the length of her neck. "You smell just as sweet," he murmured. He sucked her earlobe into his mouth, her little sigh making the hair on the back of his neck stand up straight. "You taste the same." It was true. And it was torture. When he pressed her back, pinning her hips against the cabinets, the feel of her curves against him almost brought him to his knees.

His mouth brushed hers once, still teasing. He tilted her head back, nipping her lower lip. Her lips were so damn soft. He pulled, sucking her plump lower lip until her lips parted. The tip of her tongue…stroking the curve of his lip. *Damn.*

He groaned, leaning into her, sealing her mouth with his and sliding his tongue into the hot recesses of her mouth. Her hand tangled in his hair, anchoring him firmly so she could deepen their kiss. And she did, the touch of her satin tongue making him groan. Her sudden hunger spurred him on. He gripped her hips, lifting her onto the kitchen counter. She wrapped a leg around his waist and pulled him close—arching into him.

His kiss wasn't gentle; his tongue demonstrated exactly what he wanted from her. And the soft moan, her grip on his hair, told him she wanted it too. His hold on her hips tightened as he ground against her. He tore his mouth from hers, groaning against the hollow of her throat at the building friction between them. She cried out when his mouth latched on to her neck. He devoured her, holding her tightly, wanting more.

It had always been this way with her. All that mattered was the feel of her, her response, the way she touched him.

But as quickly as she reached for him, she withdrew. Her hold went from clinging to pushing against his chest. "Spencer," she gasped. Fighting this—fighting him. He heard her deep, unsteady inhalation as she attempted to put some space between them.

Space he didn't want. He stepped back, breathing hard.

"Spencer," she repeated. Her voice was low and husky.

He looked at her. God, he wanted her. He hurt from wanting her. He was breathing heavy and losing control. He knew it, but he couldn't apologize for it. She drove him crazy, made him lose his head. She always had.

"If we're doing this… It's one time." Her eyes bored into his. "Only once."

He frowned, cupping her face in his hands. "Once?" He'd been half expecting her to tell him to leave. Now she was telling him they were going to have sex. But only once?

"I don't want to think…" She paused, her voice unsteady. "I want to feel alive…to feel *something*."

Her words cut through him. He didn't know what had happened with her marriage. Had she been mistreated? Heartbroken? She wanted one night, nothing more. And could he handle that, with the history they had, the feelings he still harbored? He knew one thing: refusing her was impossible.

Her green eyes bored into his, waiting, searching—and hungry.

Still, he had to be sure. "Tatum, I'm not sure—"

She pressed her fingers to his lips. "If the answer's no, just say it. Otherwise, I'd rather we didn't do much talking."

He raised an eyebrow. Because talking meant thinking. And she'd already made it clear she didn't want to overthink this. He *should* tell her no and walk away. Instead, he was going to give her what she wanted, what he wanted. "I'm not saying no." He tilted her head back, making sure she was listening. "You want me to kiss you, Tatum? To touch you?" he asked.

Her eyes widened. "Yes." The quiver in her voice shook him, stirring a possessiveness he hadn't felt since they were young and in love. He swallowed back the wash of memories—and regret—and focused on the job at hand.

She wanted to feel alive. He'd give it his all. And enjoy every damn minute of it.

His hands cupped her face, his thumbs tracing her lower lip before he pressed his mouth to hers. His lips parted hers, sealing their mouths and mixing their breaths. When she trembled, he smiled, wrapping his arms around her and pulling her tight against him. She was soft and warm, moving against him and gripping his shirt. He kissed her until she was clinging to him, her body molding to his, her tongue making him dizzy. Whatever she wanted, he'd give her.

He paused long enough to turn off the stove and swing her up into his arms. She twined her arms around his neck, her fingers slipping into his hair as he carried her into the living room. He set her on her feet long enough to toss the couch cushions onto the floor in front of the fire, then knelt in front of her.

His hands settled at her waist, working the fabric of her top free from the waist of her leggings. Her skin contracted beneath his fingertips, quivering. He looked up at her as his mouth brushed across her bare abdomen. She gasped, her fingers running through his hair. His lips skimmed her stomach, her waist. Her fingers tightened, tugging. He was mesmerized by the wonder on her face and the feel of her skin. Soft as silk. His hands slid up her sides and around her back, his fingers exploring every bump of her spine.

Her hands moved, settling on his shoulders to fist in the fabric of his shirt.

He lifted her hands, kissing each finger before pulling his shirt off. Her reaction was unexpected. He wanted her to touch him, hoped she would. Instead, she stared at him, slowly dropping to her knees. Her breathing was erratic, so rapid he worried she'd hyperventilate. Her hands stayed put, pressed flat against her thighs.

"Breathe, Tatum," he whispered.

She nodded, staring at his chest.

"You okay?" he asked.

She nodded, still staring at his chest.

Tatum had never shied away from telling him what she wanted. There'd been times he'd had to put on the brakes. But now she seemed hesitant. "Want me to put my shirt back on?"

She shook her head. *"No,"* she croaked.

"Talk to me," he encouraged, taking her hand. How many times had they ended up twined together, too caught up to know where one ended and the other began? It had been natural between them, easy. But now she seemed uncertain and it tore him up inside. "Tell me what you want. What you like."

She looked at him, blinking rapidly, but said nothing.

He pressed her hand against his chest. Her gaze fixed on her hand, her lips parting as her fingers traced the valley between his pectorals. "Whatever you want, Tatum…" He couldn't finish his sentence. The way she was looking at him made it impossible for him to say a word.

Her breathing echoed in the quite room, her attention focused solely on his bare chest and stomach. He was spellbound by the fascination on her face.

One second she was sitting there, facing him, her touch tentative. The next he was lying back on the pile of pillows, her hesitation replaced by desperate curiosity. He watched her expression, aware of every move her hands and fingers made. She bent over him, her long golden hair spilling onto his stomach as her lips and tongue explored the super-sensitized flesh of his nipple.

He reached up to thread his fingers in her hair, absorbing every caress and stroke. She took her time, exploring every inch of him with her soft hands and mouth. Her teeth nipped his side, her nails ran the length of his arms, and she kissed and sucked her way down his abdomen. He could barely breathe. Her tongue dipped into his belly button and he arched into her, groaning as her warm mouth brushed across his skin. "Dammit, Tatum."

She unfastened his pants, clasping the waist of his jeans and tugging his boxers off with them. She sat back on her heels then, staring at his prominent erection. No way could she miss the way he was throbbing, aching, for her. He shuddered as her fingers lightly stroked the length of him. But the noise she made, a strange broken cry, drew his focus back to her.

She tugged her shirt off, standing to remove her pants. She wavered on unsteady legs, so he sat up and helped her frantically peel off the two pairs of leggings and more socks. When she was as naked as he was, he had to touch her. He buried his face against her side, pressing a kiss against the swell of her hip, before pulling her down with him. Her lips found his, their tongues touching and stroking. He slid his hand through her hair, holding her close, savoring the taste of her as every curve and angle of her body fitted against his.

He didn't know how much more he could take. He needed her, needed to be inside of her, now. But that wouldn't be fair. He'd barely touched her. He wanted to touch her. And clearly, she needed to be touched. He wanted to make her fall apart, to lose control, to find a release. Again and again.

His hand cupped her breast, drawing her nipple deep into his mouth. She made that strange little cry again. He looked at her, at the way she bit her lower lip.

"I want to hear you," he murmured. "I want to know when you like something."

He rolled her nipple between his fingers and thumb, watching her. His tongue flicked the tip. She groaned, crying out when his mouth latched on to the other nipple.

He lifted her arms over her head, kissing along her sides, sucking the skin until he knew he'd leave marks. His hands were busy too, stroking the curve of her hip, the underside of her breast, the soft skin of her inner thigh. When his fingers traced the slick flesh between her legs, she made that strangled cry.

"Don't hold back, Tatum," he demanded, stroking the nub of nerves at her core. "Not with me." His finger parted her, sliding deep. He groaned at the feel of her, closing his eyes at her tight heat gloving his finger. He moved, stroking her skin, filling her. His thumb set an urgent rhythm against the taut bud, his finger doing the job his body ached to do. And the sounds she made... Pure torture.

Her hands gripped his shoulders as she arched into his touch. He cupped her breast, gently running his teeth over the tip as he added another finger. She was so tight around him. He groaned, burying his face against her breast and gritting his teeth against the need to bury himself inside of her. "You feel so good." He all but growled the words.

She cried out, long and ragged. He watched her face as her body contracted around his fingers. She grabbed his arm, holding his hand in place as she rode out her climax. It was the sexiest damn thing he'd ever seen. She was beautiful. So damn beautiful. And he wanted to see that look, that stunned, frantic release, on her face again.

She opened her eyes, gasping. "That was so...*so* much better than a vibrator."

He was so surprised, he laughed. And then she was laughing too.

3

TATUM STARED AT the boxes of decorations she'd pulled from the attic. They'd been buried, covered in junk and a layer of dust. But now the wreath hung over the fireplace, its colored glass balls aglow from the white lights inside. The Christmas village was arranged on the side table and she'd unpacked the train that would go around the Christmas tree. These were the things her father had delighted in… Seeing them made her think of him and happier times.

Now all she needed was a tree.

The repairman had arrived first thing. Nothing like working heat and electric, Christmas decorations, carols and a solid night's sleep to help dispel some of her moodiness.

Or the mind-blowing orgasm courtesy of Spencer. But last night had been wrong. A huge mistake. He'd caught her when she was vulnerable and needy… And it had been the single most erotic moment of her life.

Not that it would ever—*ever*—happen again. She'd been arguing with herself all morning. What had she been thinking? Why had things gotten so carried away?

And then she'd remember the feel of him, the things he'd done to her, and all her arguments faded away.

She'd been gasping, still clinging to him, when his cell phone chirped. His posture had changed instantly, his forehead creasing. "Shit," he'd muttered.

"Something wrong?" she'd asked, wishing she was still in touch with her inner teenager enough to ask him to stay and give her another orgasm—or two.

"Work," he'd groaned, nuzzling her breast again.

Her fingers had slipped through his tangled black hair. "If you ignore it, will they go away?" *Please tell me they'll go away.*

He'd chuckled, then groaned again, his breath brushing her nipples and his hand stroking along her belly. "I wish. They call, I go. *Dammit.*"

She tugged the plaid throw over her nakedness, watching him dress with a mixture of appreciation and disappointment. In that moment, disappointment won. She hadn't wanted him to go. From the bulge in his pants, she knew he didn't want to go. And when he'd looked at her, there was no denying how badly he wanted to stay. He'd kissed her, once, so hard and deep she moaned. Which made him mutter *"Dammit"* again before stomping out.

She'd lain on her nest of pillows hoping he'd reappear. But he hadn't come back and she'd eventually crawled into her bed, buried in quilts and oh so lonely.

She'd woken up with the echo of his fingers on her skin. She could still feel him, taste him… All morning she'd thought of things she wished she'd done. It wasn't the regret she was expecting, but it was still regret. He'd been her own personal playground and she'd only been allowed on one ride—a ride that had been cut short.

After living in a state of denial, her body was ready

to give in, let go and thoroughly enjoy what Spencer was willing to offer her. Too bad she'd said once.

Of course, they hadn't actually slept together so…

No. God no. What was she thinking?

"Tatum?" She heard the singsong voice through her front door. "Are you decent? It's Mrs. Ryan, dear, from across the street."

She blushed. Spencer's mother. "Coming," she called out, smoothing her red tunic into place and running a quick hand over her hair and the long beaded necklace she wore. Appearance was important. First her mother, then Brent had insisted she always look her best. And now that Spencer's mother was on the front porch, she was glad of it.

She pulled open the door to find Mrs. Ryan and Lucy Ryan, Spencer's cousin. Lucy was the one person she'd kept in contact with from Greyson—the one person Tatum had always counted a true friend. But after Lucy had come to visit her and Brent, their emails and phone calls grew further apart. Brent hadn't liked Lucy and made it clear he didn't approve of their friendship. And, sadly, Tatum hadn't fought to preserve or defend their friendship.

"Tatum!" Lucy squealed, her gray eyes widening at the sight of her.

"Lucy? Oh, Lucy," she answered, laughing when Lucy hugged her tight.

"I hadn't heard from you in a while." Lucy's voice was muffled. "It's so good to see you."

"I'm sorry," she murmured. "I guess I've sort of been in hiding."

Lucy let go of her and Mrs. Ryan hugged her gently.

"Well, you're home now and that's all that matters," the older woman said.

"We brought you cookies," Lucy said, offering her a huge basket overflowing with cookies, breads, some wine and fruit.

"Well...thank you," Tatum said, taking the basket. "Come in, please."

That was when she saw Spencer coming up the path. It hadn't been her imagination. He really was the hottest thing she'd seen in real life. And watching him stroll up her path, all bad boy and muscled body... The phantom heat of his fingers inside her body had her throbbing for his touch and aching for more. Sticking to "once" was going to be hard.

Especially if one of them didn't move out.

"Hurry up, Spencer," Lucy called. "It's cold."

Spencer took the steps two at a time, striding into the living room before Tatum could react. He hugged her, casually, his scent flooding her nostrils. "Morning, Tatum," he said tightly, his blue eyes staring into hers.

She nodded, reeling from the effect of his quick embrace.

"Well, come sit, tell us everything," Mrs. Ryan said, patting the couch beside her. "I haven't seen you in... Goodness, how long has it been?"

"Almost eight years?" Lucy asked, sitting on the couch beside her aunt.

Tatum nodded.

"You look just the same." Mrs. Ryan smiled. "I always thought we'd see you in a magazine or a movie someday."

"Oh...no." Tatum shook her head. "Would you like something to drink—"

"No, Aunt Imogene is literally bursting to ask you

questions about everything that's happened since you left," Lucy cut in.

Imogene Ryan's eyes went round. "Lucy," she chastised.

"It's true," Spencer added.

Tatum laughed, sitting in the rocking chair. She tried not to pay attention to Spencer as he knelt in front of the fire to add more logs. Tried not to think about how he'd stripped her down on the floor where her feet now rested… "Ask away," Tatum answered unsteadily.

"What have you been up to?" Mrs. Ryan asked. "I know you finished out high school in California with your father, but after that? Lucy said you went to college there?"

"UCLA," she said, shrugging. "Got my accounting degree. I get numbers." *People, not so much.*

"Ugh." Lucy winced. "No, thank you."

"Okay, Miss PhD," Tatum teased. "I met Brent there. We were married for three years. I was his wife, his accountant and his events planner…and we've been *officially* divorced for eight months."

"I'm so sorry," Mrs. Ryan said.

"I am too," she agreed. "Wish I'd had the sense to get out sooner." She smiled, trying to make light of the situation. But it was true. She'd worked hard to be what Brent wanted, keeping his books sound, his house tidy and his parties memorable. When he hired "more seasoned professionals" to do his books, the slight daily contact they had was gone. Things had disintegrated by their second anniversary. So why had she held on?

She felt Spencer's gaze on her and glanced his way. He was studying her, looking for something. But what exactly? Instead of worrying about what he was thinking or feeling, she'd be wise to remember he'd been the first one to replace her with another woman.

Whatever spark remained was purely sexual. Which was fine.

"Good riddance," Lucy chimed in. "His loss."

"That's sweet of you to say," she laughed, even if it sounded a little forced.

"It's true," Mrs. Ryan agreed. "You'll find the man that deserves you, don't you fret."

So not fretting. Worrying over her romantic future wasn't on her top-ten-things-to-worry-over list. She didn't know who she was or what she wanted—now wasn't the time to fall in love. No, that was the main reason it had fallen apart with Brent: he defined too much of her. That, and he'd been screwing the most successful real-estate agent in their wealthy, gossipy group of friends.

If anything, she didn't want a relationship right now. She needed to figure things out, needed to live a little and try new things—for herself.

Like sex. Last night had been a revelation. She *wanted* lots of hot sex. But she only knew one person she was attracted to. She glanced at Spencer again.

Could she get up the nerve to really consider such a thing? Roommates with benefits? *And* ask him if he was interested. The potential for rejection gnawed on her insides.

But last night. She drew in an unsteady breath, flooded with a tangle of want-inducing images, sensations and sounds. They *were* already sleeping under the same roof. Neither of them was involved. And, hell, they were both adults.

He could say no. She swallowed, tearing her gaze from him.

"What are your plans?" Lucy asked. "Whatever they are, tell me you're staying."

She nodded. "Come home, regroup, get a job…start again."

"Sounds like a good plan, dear," Mrs. Ryan said. "Oh, I know. I'll check in with George Welch, see if he knows of any openings in his office. He has the largest accounting firm in the county."

Tatum held up her hand. "You don't have to—"

"No, she doesn't. But it's what she does," Spencer said. "With or without your blessing, trust me."

Tatum smiled at him, then Mrs. Ryan. "Thank you."

"Free today?" Lucy asked. "I'd love to spend some time with you."

"I'd love that too," she agreed. "Up for shopping? I have no food." She paused, looking at the huge goodie basket on the table. "Well, I do now. But I'm thinking a Christmas tree might brighten things up."

"You *do* decorate?" Mrs. Ryan asked. "I'm so glad. I know your mother… Well, I'm glad."

"I do," she said. "And I want this Christmas to be extra special."

"You've got a great yard, Tatum," Spencer said.

"You had ideas for a theme, didn't you?" Lucy asked.

"Spencer, you're going to have to find a place to stay now that Tatum is back. I'm sure the last thing she wants is a roommate. Especially in your line of work. I tell you, a police officer is never off duty. Constant interruptions. Calls in the middle of the night. Never a dull moment," Mrs. Ryan said and wrinkled her nose for emphasis.

Law enforcement. It made sense. Spencer's father and grandfather had both been cops. Why shouldn't Spencer? It also explained why he left for work in the middle of the night and why he'd been on assignment for so long. She'd been too lost in a lust-induced haze to find out what he did for a living—about his life now.

Spencer sighed. "I'll figure something out."

"I feel bad to cause problems, especially this close to the holidays," Tatum jumped in. She did feel bad, which she didn't like, for forcing him out of his home, even if it was her house. And if—*if*—she did decide to proposition Spencer, it would be a hell of a lot more convenient if he was here.

Spencer's gaze met hers. "There's nothing to feel bad about."

Had his eyes always been so blue? So...unrelenting?

"I love it when people put up trees outside." Lucy steered the conversation back toward decorating. "Ooh, or those giant light-up nutcrackers?"

"Nutcrackers?" Mrs. Ryan didn't look pleased with the suggestion.

"My car's too small for that," Tatum said, eyeing the space in front of the window and remembering her father's pleasure in big, flocked trees that made a mess but looked bright and cheery glowing with colored lights.

"I can take you," Spencer offered. "To get a tree, I mean. Or two. One for inside, one for outside."

"He's got the truck," Lucy agreed. "It can fit all three of us, right?"

She caught the arched eyebrow he turned on Lucy before he answered, "Yes."

"Can't you shave before you go out in public?" Mrs. Ryan sighed heavily. "You'll have to excuse his appearance. I can't stand it when he's undercover, putting himself in harm's way. Not only is it dangerous, but he looks like a...a gang member." She waved at her son.

Tatum grinned. All she saw was a powerfully built man, a man with an amazing body and equally amazing hands. "He did surprise me last night." She felt delightfully wicked as she added, "I was a little shell-shocked when he left."

Spencer looked at her, blue eyes narrowing. "Oh, it was mutual, believe me."

The look in his eyes made her tingle. She'd been more than satisfied, even if he hadn't. But was he still interested? She hoped he was. She cleared her throat, her voice tight as she asked, "Next time, maybe we can finish our conversation?"

She saw him swallow, the flare of his nostrils, the absolutely gorgeous ridge of his jaw locking. His nod was stiff—but it was enough to have her throbbing.

"Oh, to be a fly on the wall for that conversation," Lucy murmured.

She and Spencer looked at Lucy in unison, making Lucy grin widely.

"Well, I have to get those pies in the oven for the women's auxiliary auction Saturday night." Mrs. Ryan stood. "You'll come, won't you, Tatum?"

"I'd like that, thank you," Tatum agreed.

"There are so many wonderful parties and events this time of year. *And* a wedding. A wedding you will be shaving for, Spencer?"

Spencer sighed, then nodded.

"Well, that's something, I suppose. Have fun today. Now that you're back, Tatum, I expect to see a lot more of you. You'll feel at home again in no time."

"I will, thanks," Tatum agreed.

"Good." Mrs. Ryan kissed her on the cheek. "Spencer,

make sure you get the rest of Tatum's lights done today, as well. The roof looks a little bare."

Tatum might want to strip Spencer down and explore every inch of him with her hands and mouth, but she could decorate her own house. "I can probably—"

"I'll do it," Spencer assured her. "And we'll have time to finish that conversation."

So many delicious images raced through her mind that every inch of her tightened with anticipation.

"Sounds like that's settled. You make sure the job is done right, Spencer," Mrs. Ryan said, shooting her son a stern look.

"I'll make sure," he said, staring into the fireplace, his jaw tight.

"I'll see you tomorrow, dear," Mrs. Ryan called out, waving goodbye as she headed back across the street to her house.

"She hasn't changed a bit," Tatum said, smiling at Lucy and Spencer. "You're lucky to have her."

Lucy hugged her. "Oh, Tatum... I just realized... I'm sorry about your dad. And your mom. Well, that's it. You're going to be a Ryan this Christmas, no arguing. No way you're going to spend it alone, you hear me?" She hugged her tighter. "This Christmas does need to be extra special."

Tatum blinked back her tears. She'd lost her mother and grandparents years ago. Her father had passed last year. And now, without Brent, she had no one to cele-brate with. "Thanks, Lucy. But I don't want to invade—"

"Invade," Spencer said. "You'll appreciate coming home to a quiet house." He smiled at her, his blue eyes so blue.

"Off to the tree farm?" Lucy asked. "Or would you rather go shopping?"

One look Spencer's way told her exactly what she wanted, even if it wasn't one of her choices. But she could wait. Anticipation was a good thing. Until then, she'd have to find a way to occupy herself. "Let's start with a tree."

"I'll get the truck," Spencer said, heading out the front door.

"What's it been? One day?" Lucy asked as soon as they were alone. "How naked did you get last night? And don't even try to deny it. You two—in the same room—wow. I need a fan and some ice water to cool down."

She should argue, but she'd never been good at lying. "I admit, he's… I'm…overwhelmed."

Lucy laughed. "Yeah, well, you're not alone. He almost poured orange juice in his coffee this morning."

"He did not," she argued, delighted to know their time together had him just as rattled as she was.

"Yep," Lucy said. "Aunt Imogene texted him to come straight over after work, ready to tear into him for not having the house done. I don't think he's had a break in a few weeks but his mom gets all crazy over the holidays. All he said was he'd gotten distracted. By you. Then he stormed off for a shower. I can only imagine what that meant." Lucy giggled but didn't ask questions. One of the many reasons Tatum had always loved Lucy—she didn't pry.

But Lucy's words ramped up her excitement level. If he'd found last night distracting, she couldn't wait for tonight.

SPENCER HELD HIS breath as Tatum bent forward to inspect the bin of wood-chip angels. She had great legs. Long, trim, encased in tall black boots. The sight of her round ass hugged by skintight leggings almost made him groan. It definitely made his pants uncomfortable. He shoved his hands in his pockets.

"These are adorable." She straightened, holding up one of the ornaments.

"They're to go on your outside tree," Lucy explained. "To give it that rustic look. If that's what you're going for?"

Tatum turned the ornament in her hands, her expression assessing. "I have no idea what I'm going for, but I like them."

"Start with a tree," he offered.

She looked at him, nodding. Her gaze fell to his mouth. "Whatever you say," she said.

She was teasing him. Driving him out of his damn mind. Later, he'd remind her she said that. All he could think about was getting her back to her place and into her bed. Instead, he barked out, "This way," and led them outside. If he was lucky, the chill in the air would help him gain some control over his libido. The last time he'd felt this kind of desire, he'd been nineteen and she'd been his whole world. He glanced back at her, talking and laughing with Lucy. He was older, more grounded now…but somehow being around her made him forget that.

Last night had been a revelation. Leaving her had been one of the hardest things he'd ever done. Yes, he'd wanted to finish what they'd started, but it was more than that. They'd had unfinished business for a long time. Now that she was back, and they were the way they still were, he hoped he'd finally be able to apologize. And, if she'd give him the chance, explain why he'd done what he did—why he'd broken both of their hearts. His had never fully recovered.

One hour and two trees later, they were pulling in front of Tatum's house. He was glad Lucy had volunteered to squeeze in the middle. He'd spent most of the day being aware of Tatum's every move. He wasn't sure how he'd react if he was being pressed up against her. His wayward body had no problem revealing just how much he wanted her. Walking through a Christmas tree farm with a hard-on wasn't exactly socially acceptable but there hadn't been a damn thing he could do about it. Now that they were back at her place and he knew what he had to look forward to, he was in for a long, uncomfortable evening.

Spencer followed them down the path, watching the light fall of snowflakes settle in Tatum's hair. She was shivering. Didn't she have a heavy coat? Guess it didn't get too cold in Los Angeles. It took everything he had not to pull her close and warm her up.

As Tatum opened the front door, Lucy said, "If you decide you need extra hands, call my brothers Dean and Jared. They're off tomorrow. I figure Zach is going to be pretty out-of-pocket since this is his first Christmas as a married man. And with Patton's wedding coming up—"

"Zach is married?" Tatum asked, stunned. "Is Patton finally marrying Ellie? She was so stuck on him." She hung her keys on a hook by the door.

"Patton and Ellie ended a while back," Spencer said. "Cady, Patton's fiancée, she's a force of nature. One my brother didn't stand a chance against."

"It was one of those whirlwind sort of things," Lucy agreed. "The wedding's New Year's Eve at a fancy mountaintop resort in Colorado that Zach manages. Romantic, right?"

Her open disbelief had Spencer grinning from ear to ear. "Really?"

Spencer nodded. "I know. Patton. Whirlwind. Marriage. Romance. Who'd have thought?" His big brother Patton was hardly the hearts and flowers type. Hell, neither was Zach. But somehow they were both content to be tied to one woman.

Tatum nodded. "He was always sort of...stuffy. And reserved. No offense."

"None taken. He was. Hell, for the most part, he still is." Spencer laughed.

Lucy giggled. "You should see him, Tatum. He's adorable. Never in a million years did I think Patton could be so crazy in love. And show it. But Cady's got him hooked."

"It's nauseating," Spencer agreed. But that wasn't really true. He was happy for his brothers—hell, he envied them. Both of them had the love of a good woman, women who completed them.

"And Zach?" Tatum asked.

"Bianca," Lucy said. "Sweetest girl I have ever met. I think we were all worried he'd bring home some world-traveling, socialite type with his career and all. But Bianca is wonderful, grounded and kind. You'll meet them both soon, being an honorary Ryan this year."

He saw the look on Tatum's face, the yearning pressing in on him.

"I remember being so jealous of you growing up," Tatum said, hooking her arm with Lucy's. "A big family, get-togethers, big parties." Her gaze met his. "There was always something happening at your house, Spencer.

Lots of laughter. And they're all still here? Your whole family?" Tatum asked. "That's—"

"Smothering?" he interjected, laughing.

Tatum laughed.

"Sometimes," Lucy agreed. "But when you've got multiple trees to decorate and a mother who wanted this done yesterday, having extra hands—"

"Is pretty damn convenient," Spencer agreed.

"So, tomorrow, we'll get you set up before the big Holiday Lights kickoff?" Lucy asked. "I'd offer to stay and help tonight, but I promised to watch Mrs. Medrano's grandson."

Which was a relief. He didn't know how he was going to get Lucy to leave, but there was no way he and Tatum wanted a chaperone tonight. He grinned, anticipation warming his blood. "I'll get the house lights done. And the tree up." He glanced at Tatum, noting the flush to her cheeks and hoping it meant she was just as eager. "What else do you want to tackle tonight, Tatum?"

The look she shot him made him bite back a hiss. Damn, but her face gave everything away. And damn if he didn't like the way her mind was working.

"Shopping," Lucy prompted.

Tatum nodded, tearing her gaze from his. "Yes. Food... I should go to the store. You're doing so much to help me out, the least I can do is feed you. And your family tomorrow."

"I'll get started here," he agreed.

Lucy checked her watch. "I have an hour. We can shop, I'll drop you off and head to Mrs. Medrano's?"

"Thank you," Tatum said. "Thank you both for today. It was great to get out, to have...fun doing normal things, you know?"

He needed to remember she'd been through a hell of a lot. She seemed happy, but then, Tatum had always been the smiling, upbeat sort—even when she was hurting on the inside. He wanted her to *be* happy. If Lucy wasn't standing here, he'd tell her as much. She deserved to be happy. And if chopping down a tree and putting up some lights made her happy, he'd do it.

He was also more than willing to take off all her clothes, spread her out on her bed and love her body until she was shouting his name. He knew that would make him very happy. He shoved his hands back in his pockets.

Lucy hugged her. "It's Christmas, Tatum. You're home. You should be happy."

Tatum's smile touched his heart. He'd missed her. He'd missed that smile.

"Now let's go get you some food so you're not starving," Lucy said. "Need anything?" she asked him.

"Nope."

Lucy nodded and headed out the door.

Tatum smiled up at him. "You sure you don't want anything?"

"You know I do. But we've got all night," he promised, his gaze shifting to her full red lips. "And I plan on taking advantage of that."

She shivered. "Who said last night's offer was still good?"

He smiled. "It's still good."

She opened her mouth, then closed it. Her green eyes narrowed before she whispered, "I'll hurry."

He nodded, taking in every nuance of her reaction. The dilated pupils, flushed cheeks, parted lips, the quickening of her breath... When their eyes locked, he wanted to lose himself in her—to bury himself deep and never come up for air.

"Tatum?" Lucy called from the front porch.

She blinked, smiled up at him and headed out the door.

He stood watching them run across the snow-covered lawn to Lucy's waiting car.

Loving Tatum had been as easy and natural as breathing. They'd been inseparable, snatching every spare moment together. How many nights had he scaled the side of the house to meet her on her roof? How many nights had they lain there, staring up at the stars and sharing their plans? Plans he'd severed for her. To protect her. Even though driving her away had made every day for the next two years an exercise in survival. He swallowed, watching Lucy's car pull away from the curb.

Now they had time, time he wanted with her. So he needed to get the damn lights up.

He worked quickly. First things first, he dragged her tree inside, ready to decorate. Then he worked outside, finishing the roof and dormer windows, wrapping the rest of the porch railings and hanging lights around the front windows. He stood back, looking up at his handiwork.

"You're a Christmas light superhero." Tatum's voice reached him.

He glanced back to see her, holding two large bags of groceries. "Got it?"

"There's two more," she said. "If you can grab them, Lucy can head to Mrs. Medrano's. I think I made her late."

"I think Mrs. Medrano can be five minutes late for her weekly bingo game," Spencer said, hoping to reassure her. "But I'll get the groceries."

"Thanks." She hurried toward the front door.

He opened the back door of Lucy's car.

"You okay?" Lucy asked him.

He frowned at her. "Why wouldn't I be?"

"Don't get all defensive. I'm not being your shrink—I'm being your cousin. The one that knows how devastated you were after your breakup and Tatum left, remember? So I'm worried about you, sue me." Lucy sighed. "What is it with men acting like they have no emotions? Like it's some weakness or something. News flash—women like men that emote. Not cry their eyeballs out, but emote."

Spencer laughed. "Okay, I'll try to remember that." He paused. "I'm good. I'm glad she's back."

Lucy nodded. "I thought you might be."

He scooped the two bags of groceries from the back. "Have fun tonight."

"You too," she said, giggling. "I'm pretty sure you're not going to need this, but here. In case you need my sofa to sleep on." She held out a key.

He hoped she was right, that he wouldn't need it, but he took it anyway. "Thanks." He slammed the car door and headed back to the house. It looked good. No one on the neighborhood decorating committee could complain now—his mother included. He pushed through the front door, gently shoving the door shut behind him. He put the groceries on the counter and placed the eggs and milk in the refrigerator before he saw Tatum's shopping bags sitting—unpacked—on the counter.

"Tatum?" he called out.

No answer.

He headed down the hall, toward her room. "Tatum?"

He knocked, pushing her door open to find it empty. That was when he heard the telltale sound of water running. She was in the shower? He went back out into the hall and paused. The bathroom door was cracked. He'd take that as an invitation.

He opened the door, greeted by a cloud of steam, and pushed it closed behind him. Her red tunic lay on the floor. Her leggings, boots, a lacy black bra and a scrap of fabric he assumed was her underwear led the way to the glass-enclosed shower.

"You hoping I'd wash your back?" he asked, his throat tight.

She glanced over her shoulder, smiling sweetly. "To start, maybe."

"To start?" he asked.

"You said we had all night." He heard the waver of her voice and knew she wasn't as brave as she was acting.

He nodded and stripped quickly, leaving his clothes in a pile on the floor before stepping into the shower behind her. He stepped forward, shuddering as he pressed against her. There was no way she could miss just how much he wanted her. The length of him was throbbing, pulsing against the soft curve of her ass. He leaned in, his chest flush with the wet skin of her back. He groaned as he pressed an openmouthed kiss against the base of her neck.

She shivered.

He reached around her, pouring body wash into his palm and lathering his hands. His palms slid up her arms and over her shoulders. He took his time, kneading her skin with strong fingers. She sighed, her head falling against his shoulder as he massaged the length of her back. He washed her, his hands slipping and sliding over every inch of her. He didn't linger in one place, but used his touch to heighten her awareness...and his. His hand slid between her legs, barely cupping the soft skin before sliding up her stomach to cradle her breasts. Her nipples were tight peaks, begging for his touch. He almost caved, pushed her against the wall and slid home. But he didn't. Not yet. She felt so damn good, the lather of the body wash making her slippery in his hold. When his hands clasped her hips, he ground against her.

Her hand came around, gripping his lower back as she arched into him. She turned her head, looking at him with unfiltered hunger.

She turned in his hold, pressing herself against him and twining her arms around his neck. Her teeth nipped his lower lip, her fingers curling in his hair to pull his head toward hers. He didn't hold back. His tongue slid between her lips while his mouth sealed hers.

She broke away, gasping. "My turn." She poured body wash onto her hands.

He stood still, watching as she explored his body with her hands and eyes. She turned him, kneading his back and shoulders, thighs and hips. Her teeth grazed his hips, her tongue traced his spine, and her hands came around him, clasping the length of him with slippery hands. He shuddered, giving in to the onslaught of sensations her hands and mouth unleashed. She turned him once more.

He hadn't expected her to be on her knees, to have her soft hands clasp the rigid length of him and bring it to her mouth. But the silk of her lips slipping over his tip, the wet heat of her mouth encasing him, made him groan out loud. With one hand she braced herself on his thighs, and the other gripped him firmly in place, letting her set a rhythm both sweet and torturous. Every stroke of her tongue and caress of her lips had him teetering closer to the edge. Did she know how close he was? He pressed his hands against the side of the shower, steadying himself.

"Stop, Tatum," he ground out. He had to stop her. Had to get control. But, when it came to Tatum, he had no control.

"Stop?" she asked, breathless. "You're not enjoying it?"

He heard the vulnerability in her voice and ached from it. He groaned. "I am. Too much."

"I don't want to stop," she answered, drawing him deep into her mouth. Her hands slid up the backs of his thighs to grip his hips and he was done for. His climax hit hard. Wave after wave of pure, raw pleasure rocked through him. His moan tore from his throat and echoed in the steam-filled shower.

When he opened his eyes, she was standing before him—a huge smile on her face. He was gasping, his heart hammering and his lungs scrambling for air. She seemed pretty proud of her handiwork.

His hands slid down the side of the shower stall to cup her face. He wiped the water from her forehead and tilted her face back to kiss her. "You're gorgeous," he said, pressing a kiss to her forehead.

"I probably look like a drowned rat," she argued, kissing him back.

"A gorgeous drowned rat," he continued, pulling her against him. He groaned at the slip and slide of her skin against him.

"Spencer." Her whisper was low, pleading.

He held her back, staring down at her. "Bed?" he asked, turning off the water without waiting for her answer.

He helped her out of the shower, wrapping a thick white towel around his waist before rubbing her down.

She laughed at the thorough job he made of it, but she was dry and rosy when he was done.

Her fingers traced his side. "What kind of feather is this?" she asked, tracing the tattoo.

"An eagle feather," he answered, twisting the water from her hair.

"Why an eagle feather?"

He glanced at her. "An eagle is a protector. He's powerful in battle. Alert and watchful. I needed to feel that way after Russ was killed." Instead of feeling like a failure.

He and Patton had worked side by side with their little brother but neither of them had ever suspected Russell of being corrupt. Even after the night Russ was mowed down, Spencer had a hard time coming to terms with the truth. His little brother had been the bad guy.

Tatum was staring up at him, her fingers stroking the intricately detailed design and easing the crushing weight of his memories.

"I'm sorry about Russ." There was no doubting her sincerity. "He was a character, always the jokester."

She was right. Russ had always been the class clown—the one everybody loved. Being charming was a very useful way to divert suspicion.

"To lose your brother and father in the same year..." She paused, sliding her arms around his waist. "I'm sorry you had so much grief all at once, Spencer."

He stared down at her, loving the feel of her in his arms. *Missing her.* How many times had he picked up the phone to call her, only to hang up? "Things were tough for a while," he admitted. "But you get up every day, you find a way to keep going."

She nodded. "You have to." Her voice was thick.

There was a sheen to her eyes. She knew all about grief. She'd lost everyone she'd ever loved. If he could chase away her suffering he would. So he kissed her, a long, slow kiss that instantly stirred his desire. "I'm glad you're back, Tatum."

"I'm thinking my stunt in the shower might have something to do with that," she teased.

"I'm not complaining," he murmured.

Her green eyes searched his before she said, "My body feels awake when you're around. *I* feel awake." Her fingers stroked across his chest and down his stomach.

"It's a damn good thing because I'm not planning on getting much sleep tonight." He scooped her up in his arms and carried her out the door and down the hall to her bedroom.

4

TATUM WATCHED THE lone drop of water run down Spence's neck. Even his neck was muscular. He was one hard, rippling mass of sheer power. And yet, wrapped in his arms, she felt only safe and secure—almost treasured. And there was no denying the hunger he had for her. She wanted him crazy for her, the way she was crazy for him. She bent forward, licking the drop of water from his skin.

She landed in the middle of her bed, the cool air hitting her exposed skin—right before his hands clasped her hips and tugged her to the edge of the bed. She was still reeling when his tongue stroked over the tight bundle of nerves between her legs.

"Spencer," she hissed, her hands fisting in the blankets beneath her.

"Turnabout is fair play," he murmured, his warm breath brushing along the inside of her thigh.

His tongue was magic, teasing her until she was out of her mind. His fingers joined in then, stroking deep inside of her. He moved with a purpose, setting a rhythm that was both blissful and maddeningly taunting. It built, her need, until she couldn't hold on.

"Please, Spencer," she gasped, so close. "Oh, please." She reached for him, her hands holding on to his wet hair. His rhythm stayed the same, but the pressure… His mouth, his fingers pushed her over the edge. Her body spiraled, her lungs emptying of all air as she gave way to sensation. Her grip tightened on his hair as her climax found her. She lay, shuddering and stunned, as he kissed his way back up her body.

She was still reeling when his lips pressed against hers. She felt him, hard and ready, against her thigh. Her gaze met his, the heat of his hunger making her quiver once more. He was big…bigger than Brent. And she wanted him, all of him. Now. "I'm ready," she whispered, her fingers gripping his arms.

"Protection… In my pants, in the bathroom."

"I'm protected." Her hands tightened on his arms.

"I've waited so long, I can wait a while longer," he murmured against her lips.

"Why?" she asked, wrapping a leg around his hip.

He smiled down at her, his hands cradling the side of her face. "Maybe I want to drive you crazy for me."

"You have," she answered, her heart in her throat. She could feel him, so close. "I want you, Spencer."

His eyes fluttered closed before he gripped her hips and lifted her, opening her for him. When his eyes met hers, he moved into her, slowly filling her. She gasped, her hands resting on his chest as she concentrated on relaxing. Her body strained to accommodate him, the pressure building and emptying her lungs. She closed her eyes, sucking in a deep breath.

"Tatum," he growled, stilling. "Look at me." His hands tightened on her hips.

She did. The look on his face was almost pained. He

thrust deep, so deep, never breaking their gaze. She cried out, unable to stop herself. It was too much. Too good. Too intimate. She wanted more. He thrust again, his raw groan forcing a soft cry from her lips.

He kissed her, his tongue caressing her own. She moved beneath him, losing herself to the feeling of him deep inside of her. The weight of him, the power… All she could do was hold on.

Her hands slid along his back, gripping his hips. The quiver and contraction of his muscles beneath her fingers, the pause at each thrust, his ragged breathing—he was barely holding on, for her. When all she wanted was all of him. She didn't want restrained or controlled. She wanted to let go, for him to let go. To give in to the passion that would undoubtedly drown them both.

"You feel so good, Tatum…so damn good," he growled. He moved deep, almost leaving her, and slid home again. Over and over, he had her so close. His mouth latched on to her neck, her shoulder, her nipple. He drew her breast into his mouth, his tongue flicking, his teeth nipping. She arched into him, everything but him fading away.

He moved faster then, lifting her and holding her in place as he powered into her. She was out of her mind, overwhelmed, balancing on the precipice of pleasure and pain. Her hands slid down his back, feeling the flex and shift of his muscles. His body was incredible. He was incredible.

One look at his face was all it took. Her pleasure slammed into her. Her body bowed off the bed, the sharp edge of pleasure giving way to a powerful climax. She was drowning in sensation. But he wasn't done.

He kept moving, harder and faster, driven. She watched

him, gasping for breath, instantly aroused by the sweet friction. "Spencer..." His name slipped from her lips, thick and husky.

His arms were columns of steel, bracing him over her as his eyes bored into hers. His face crumpled and he stiffened, shouting out his own release. She wasn't prepared for the hard climax that gripped her, making her yell out as she held on to him. Still he gripped her tightly to him, pinning her.

They collapsed in a tangled heap, panting on her quilts. He was heavy, sprawled across her. But she ached when he moved to her side. She didn't want this to end. She wanted to stay here, lost in pure passion and sensation. His arm drew her tight against his side before pulling the quilts over them and bundling them closely together.

"Warm enough?" he asked against her hair.

She nodded, loving the waver in his voice. Even now, savoring the delightful aftershocks of their lovemaking, she wanted him. It didn't matter that her body was humming, satisfied.

He chuckled.

"What?" she asked.

"You still have pom-poms on your shelf," he said, pointing at the shelf across the room.

"You live here," she said, breathing a little easier now. "You could have boxed them up."

He shook his head. "It's your room. The last tenants hadn't touched this side of the house. I didn't, either."

"Can I ask why this house?" she asked, looking up at him.

"My apartment building burned and it was empty so... I didn't like seeing the place sit empty." He shrugged.

"Sorry about your apartment." How horrible. And now she was going to make him move again.

"Thanks. It sucked." He paused. "I'm not home a lot. I didn't lose anything important. Like pom-poms or trophies."

She laughed, slightly embarrassed that her room hadn't been touched. She'd just assumed the house had been packed up for tenants—Brent had assured her that was the case. "I haven't had a chance to weed things out or decorate yet." She looked up at him. "I've spent more time naked with you."

"Again, not complaining," he said, smiling down at her. "Just a little déjà vu. Being here, in your bed, when the room looks the same."

"We never did this, never slept together," she argued. "Before."

"I know. But we spent a hell of a lot of time right here doing plenty of other things." His arms tightened around her.

His words poked at the hurt he'd caused so long ago. She'd left the middle of her senior year of high school and had only the haziest memories of her time in California high school. What she did remember was pain. Losing him had felt like losing an arm. She'd felt confused and broken.

It was only when she met Brent that she put every thought and memory of Spencer in a box, tightly latched, in the far recesses of her mind. That box needed to stay locked up. "So what have you been up to?" she asked, desperate to turn their conversation into neutral waters. "Besides busting bad guys and taking care of your mom, have you taken up any hobbies? Like woodworking or… beer making?" she asked. "You know all about me."

"I know the bare minimum," he said, tucking an arm under his head and looking down at her.

"Nothing more to tell, I guess." It was true—and pathetic. The last few years had made her a Stepford wife. Whatever thoughts she'd had or plans she'd made had been replaced by things Brent needed to get ahead in his career. She didn't want to admit that to Spencer. Especially when they were wrapped up, naked, in bed together.

His fingers slid through her hair as he spoke. "Mostly school, then the academy. I've worked my way up to detective, alongside Patton. Been in the narcotics unit for a few years now. Greyson's still pretty small, but shit happens now and then. The real action is when I'm working with the joint task force. Being so close to the Oklahoma border, with as much wide-open land as there is, we do have a lot of drug on the move."

"You're happy?" she asked, curious. She understood loving your work, but was that really enough? Spencer had always wanted a big family, like the one he'd grown up in. She'd wanted that with him… But that was a long time ago.

He nodded, reaching out to tuck a strand of her hair behind her ear. "Mostly."

"No women?" she asked.

He grinned. "Oh, there have been women."

She smacked him on the arm and sat up, tucking the sheet around her. "Relationships?"

He shrugged. "None that stuck. My job comes first. Hours aren't exactly family friendly." He broke off, staring at her. "I figure I'll know when it's the right time. Or the right girl."

"So you're not attached?" she asked.

"If I was, I wouldn't be here, Tatum." He paused. "You know me."

She thought she had. And then he'd proved her wrong. "Not really," she said, suddenly nervous.

"You do. You know me better than anyone." He frowned.

Maybe once. But now it didn't matter. She didn't want to get serious when she was about to suggest what she was about to suggest. "I have a proposition for you." What she wanted was crazy and selfish and indecent, no denying that. And without Spencer it wasn't going to happen. But she really hoped he was agreeable to her proposal. "I want to…borrow you," she said, her voice lowered.

"Borrow me?" he asked.

She swallowed. "Your body. It was just Brent, and he was…well… I just wanted… I was wondering if you'd be willing to help me… Learn to be sexy. Appealing… in bed."

His blue eyes continued to stare at her, intense and searching.

"No strings. I'm not ready and you sound like you're not interested in getting tied down, which is great. But I feel like I've missed out… On sex—good sex. I want to be sexy…seductive." She stopped, clasping her hands in her lap. Maybe she should have kept her mouth shut. Saying it out loud, she sounded ridiculous.

He lay there, still staring at her. His breathing had accelerated, but she didn't know what that meant.

"You can stay here. Roommates with benefits." She swallowed again, her nerves forcing her to continue. "You and me, two consenting adults, spending as much time naked as possible. With an expiration date of midnight Christmas Eve."

He frowned. "Why Christmas Eve?"

"I'm supposed to fly to a friend's on the West Coast Christmas day," she explained.

His eyes narrowed slightly. "Two weeks?"

"Twelve days," she clarified.

"Like the Christmas carol?" He smiled.

"With less birds and more sex, sure," she agreed, laughing.

"What do you mean you need me to help you feel sexy or appealing?" he asked.

She shrugged, wishing she hadn't shared that piece of information.

"Come on, Tatum, it's a fair question. I think you did a damn fine job seducing me in the shower. As far as I'm concerned, you're sexy as hell."

"Oh." She smiled.

His hand came up to stroke her cheek. "Only Brent?"

Another piece of information she hadn't meant to share.

"And he let you go?" His voice was rough. "Stupid shit."

So did you. But she pressed her lips tight. "I guess men are different. You *like* me to make noise, to touch you—to respond."

He frowned. "I'm pretty sure all men like that." He twined her hair around her fist and pulled her down to kiss him. "If it feels good, I want to know. Plus, it's hot."

She shuddered, leaning into him. "Is that a yes?" she asked.

He took his time inspecting her face and body. She heard the change in his breathing when his gaze fell to her breasts. And sighed as his hand cupped her, his thumb grazing the hardening peak.

"Spencer?" she asked, feeling exposed and aroused. She didn't know what she wanted more, his answer or his mouth on her body.

SPENCER LOOKED AT her face. She was so easy to excite, so responsive. To see her come alive under his touch was a powerful aphrodisiac. He couldn't get enough of her. Her body was meant for touching. And she was offering herself to him for twelve days. Twelve days of no-strings-attached sex. With Tatum.

"You think twelve days will be enough?" he asked, stroking her nipple with the pad of his thumb. She hardened beneath his touch, and she had the exact same effect on his body. He'd come twice in the last hour and he was already ready for round three.

She clasped his wrist, holding his fingers in place against her breast. "Guess we'll find out?"

He nodded, bending to kiss her. "I guess so." He kissed her until she was breathless, until her arms were wrapped around him and her fingers twisted in his hair. "I'm hungry," he said against her mouth. "I need food. If you think you can control yourself?"

She laughed, the gentle curves of her body brushing against him and threatening his resolve to wait. "I'll try." She sighed. "At least I went to the grocery store. I can feed you."

"Good idea. Don't want me to waste away." He kissed the tip of her nose.

"Not for the next twelve days, anyway," she added, slipping from the bed.

"Ouch," he teased. "Only want me for my body, huh?"

"Yes," she answered, laughing. "But I admit, I'm hungry too." She slipped into her robe, pulled the sash tight and headed into the kitchen.

He followed, in nothing but his boxer shorts. She was staring at him with such appreciation he couldn't help but grin. He ran a hand through his hair and crossed his arms over his chest. "What?"

"Just enjoying the view," she admitted.

He cocked an eyebrow. "I'm in favor of matching outfits."

She shook her head, laughing. "What sounds good?" she asked, unpacking the grocery bags.

"Whatever's quick and easy?"

"Omelet?"

They fell into step, working side by side. He watched the way she moved, how graceful and easy she was in the kitchen. "You know your way around the kitchen," he said, washing off the tomatoes.

"Lots of cooking classes. They were cheaper than hiring a caterer every time we threw some fancy dinner for one reason or another. And I liked cooking," she said with a smile, chopping up some mushrooms and tomatoes with quick, sure strokes. She stopped long enough to turn on some Christmas music, then tossed some onions in a skillet. By the time dinner was ready, his mouth was watering from the delicious aromas scenting the air.

They sat on the floor in front of the Christmas tree, enjoying their meal. He rested against the couch, propped on some pillows, savoring his beer. He watched her, her green eyes fixed on the tree. The firelight turned her eyes deep emerald and the gold of her hair shone. She hummed along with the instrumental carol playing, the only other sound the snap and pop from the fire. The night couldn't get much better.

She glanced at him. "So, Spencer, what do you want for Christmas?"

He chuckled. "My present came early this year." What more could he want?

Her brows rose, stunned. "Me?"

He laughed. Did she not realize what a treasure she was? She might be in this for the sex. He saw this as his second chance.

She shook her head. "You must have wanted something, before I came along and offered you endless sex."

He sat quietly, thinking about it. "If I did, I can't remember." It was a sobering thought. She'd only been here two days and he was already so caught up in her. Maybe this proposal was more dangerous than he realized. He took a sip of his wine. "Are you going to the charity auction?" he asked.

"I told your mom I'd go," she answered. "Guess it's time I stopped being a hermit and returned to the land of the living. I admit I'm not looking forward to the questions and comments, but I guess it's unavoidable."

"Questions and comments?" he asked.

"I thought about having a shirt made up that says something like, 'I'm divorced, I've moved back home and I'm fine.' But I wasn't sure how that would go over." She shrugged. "Most people mean well. But admitting I've already been replaced is embarrassing."

No one could replace her. He knew—he'd tried. "I never liked Brent." He smiled, watching her smile in return.

"You never met him."

"Don't have to. I don't like him." He finished off his omelet, watching her shake her head, poking at the food on her plate.

She'd always had a good attitude—that was one of the things that had drawn him to her. Even living in a less-than-happy home, Tatum had a loving heart. Living across the street, he and his brothers had heard the yelling. Jane Buchanan, Tatum's mother, had been a hard woman. Hell, most people called her The Witch Buchanan. When her husband left, Tatum had to deal with her mother's demands and unrealistic expectations on her own. Nothing Tatum did was ever good enough. Even though she'd been involved in every school club or organization, she had few real friends. No one wanted to come to her place and she was rarely let out of the house.

He'd been the one to climb onto her roof and pull her out. He'd been the one to hold her close and listen to her, support her. The connection between them had been so powerful, so out of control, it had bordered on obsession.

When her mother's behavior grew dangerous, Spencer had done the only thing he could. He couldn't stand to see her so bruised, her body and her spirit. Her father wanted her in California, away from her mother. But Tatum stayed—for Spencer. Breaking up with her took her away from her mother and the judgment of their small town. And him. She was free to start over, to flourish and have a parent that adored her, new friends and accomplishments.

"You could go with me?" he asked. "To the charity auction, I mean."

Her eyes went round. "No. No, that would make it a million times worse." She shook her head. "People would talk, assume we were involved again—"

"That we're sleeping together?" he asked, reaching for the tie on her robe. The silky fabric parted, revealing the full creamy curve of her breast. His fingers traced the swell, brushing along the tip until she pebbled beneath his fingers. He smiled.

She blew out an uneven breath. "You're teasing me."

"And loving every minute of it." He nodded, his hand falling from her. "I'll do the dishes."

She shook her head. "I won't argue."

After the kitchen was clean, he headed back to find her propped on some pillows, staring into the fire. He gazed at her, mesmerized. Twelve days of this… Christmas really had come early.

"Is that for me?" she asked, reaching for the glass of wine he'd brought her.

He nodded, sitting beside her and covering them both with her plaid throw. "What about you?"

"What about me?" she asked, looking up at him.

"What do you want for Christmas?" he asked.

"Hmm, besides having sex without something that requires batteries? I'll have to think about that."

"Go through a lot of batteries?" he asked, partly teasing. Did Brent have some sort of physical defect?

She looked up at him. "Possibly."

Just imagining her enjoying her battery-powered friend had him rock hard. "You're not going to need batteries for a while," he murmured, brushing her lips with his. "Unless you want to liven things up."

She stared at him, her cheeks turning red. "Liven things up?" she repeated softly.

"Play. Experiment," he whispered, his fingers stroking the side of her neck. "Whatever you want."

"I…I don't know."

"We'll have to work on that." His mouth latched on to her lower lip.

She shuddered. "What about you? What do you want?" Her teeth nipped his lower lip.

He hissed, pulling her onto his lap. He untied her sash and pushed the robe from her shoulders, exposing her breasts. She filled his hands, silky soft, making him ache to possess her. "Damn, Tatum, I don't know where to start," he said, his voice low and broken.

She reached down between them, freeing him from his boxers. "Let's start here," she murmured, wincing as she slid onto him. She was so hot, so tight. If he wasn't careful he'd be done before she was.

He groaned, his head falling back on the couch. "Here's good." He blew out a breath, focusing on something neutral, to keep his head. But the feel of her, like a glove...

She started slow, but soon her nails were biting into the skin of his shoulders and the feel of her ass bouncing against his thighs was too hard to fight. He looked at her, their eyes locking. He wasn't prepared for the ferocious ownership he felt. Or the desire to protect her, to cherish her. Maybe it was the hunger in her eyes, the unabashed want she had for him. But whatever it was, he knew he was in trouble. Even buried deep, he wanted more of her. His hands tangled in her hair, pulling her lips to his. He caught her cry in his mouth, wrapping his arms around her as her body shook with her release. He held her, letting her take him over the edge with her. He went, every muscle clenched tight, his body wrung dry and his lungs emptying until he was spent.

She rested her head on his shoulder, her wavering breath fanning across his chest. She'd always felt right in his arms, like she was made for him. And that was what scared him. Leaning back, he cradled her against him, worrying that these twelve days might just break his heart all over again.

5

TATUM STRETCHED AND rolled onto her side. But when she opened her eyes, she realized she was alone. She sat up. "Spencer?" she called out.

No answer. A peek at the clock told her it was eight fifteen. Sleeping in was a rarity. But after last night... She smiled, stretching with a soft squeal before collapsing back on the mattress. She stared up at the ceiling, enjoying images from last night to warm her up. Spencer. Spencer's hands and mouth and his incredible body. Last night had been... Her breathing grew a little unsteady and her heart rate picked up. How she could want him again—so fiercely—when she enjoyed him not three hours ago was a mystery. But she did.

"Spencer?" She threw back the blankets and slipped into her robe, smiling at the delectable soreness left from last night. Once her slippers were on, she headed into the kitchen. But no Spencer.

There was a brown paper bag on the counter, her name sprawled across it. She grinned as she opened the bag and found a large breakfast burrito wrapped in foil inside. And a note.

She pulled out the note and carried her burrito to the kitchen table. It read,

On the first night of Christmas, my lover took from me: sleep. But I'm not complaining. Be back with the family around 9:30 a.m.

She smiled, tucking his note in her robe pocket, and unwrapped her breakfast. On the counter, a small pot was on, heating coffee he'd obviously made and left for her. Sex all night, hot coffee and yummy food, and a sweet note. She could get used to this roommate-with-benefits thing. She munched away on the burrito and poured herself a cup of steaming coffee.

A flutter of movement caught her eye, drawing her attention to the view out the window over the kitchen sink. It was snowing, thick, heavy flakes falling steadily onto the already carpeted expanse of her backyard. Snow didn't last long in Texas. Ice and slush were more prevalent. If she'd been little she would have hurried to get dressed so she was the first person to touch the snow. She'd make snow angels and build a small snowman and make snowballs to have ready—Lucy would've come over for a snowball fight. But then the Ryan boys would sneak up on them when they were halfway through their snowman, annihilating it and burying them under a hailstorm of well-packed, well-aimed snowballs. She and Lucy would end up soaked and shivering in front of the fireplace, waiting to thaw before going out to finish their snowman.

Not this time.

The clock told her she didn't have much time. She finished off her breakfast, swallowed down the strong coffee and hurried to make stew for later. Once that was done, she fished out her baby-pink ski gear from her high school ski trip. She dressed, tugging on the faux fur–trimmed puffy coat and a knit hat with its matching pink pom-pom on top before pulling on her snow boots. She might look ridiculous, but she was warm. In no time, she was in the backyard, preparing her snowball arsenal for the arrival of the Ryan boys. She finished just in time for the telltale sound of voices in the front yard.

Tatum sneaked around the side of the house. "Lucy?" she whispered as loudly as she dared.

Lucy saw her, her eyes going round as Tatum waved her over.

Spencer, Dean and Jared had no idea what hit them. She and Lucy unleashed years of pent-up frustration, pummeling the three until their dark coats were crusty with snow. The few snowballs they managed to throw couldn't compare with the intense rain of freezing cold missiles she and Lucy kept lobbing their way.

When the last snowball was gone, she and Lucy set off at a dead run for the house—knowing their luck was done. As they pulled the door shut behind them, the re-sounding thud of at least a half a dozen snowballs hitting the door reverberated through the entry hall.

They were laughing too hard to care.

"You are a genius," Lucy said. "That was…"

"Epic," Tatum finished. "Though I suppose the nice thing to do now is make them some coffee?"

Lucy rolled her eyes. "When did they ever do anything to warm us up?"

Tatum couldn't help but remember all the wonderful things Spencer had done last night. He'd warmed her up. She was getting warm just thinking about it—and him.

Lucy was waving her hand in front of her face. "Earth to Tatum. I so don't want to know what you're thinking right now. Let's make coffee."

Five minutes later, her kitchen was filled with three shivering, irritable men holding steaming cups of coffee.

Lucy continued to giggle off and on.

But Tatum was too caught up in the bright blue gaze of Spencer, intense and brooding.

"Not the welcome I was expecting," Dean said, grinning over his coffee mug at her. "But the coffee helps."

"Oh, come on," Lucy said. "How many times did Tatum and I end up face-first in snow while you three ran off laughing?"

The three of them mumbled, knowing she was right. They gave up, grinning in defeat.

"Exactly," Lucy continued.

"Well played," Jared said, toasting her with his mug. "Might need another cup, though. My boots are full of snow and I can't feel my toes."

Tatum laughed. "Sorry."

"Somehow I don't believe that," Spencer said, his eyes pinning hers.

She couldn't say a word. The heat in his look was blazing, chasing away any of the chill that clung to her. When his gaze traveled along her neck, she could almost feel his touch on her skin.

"So how's life been treating you?" Dean asked, breaking the hold Spencer had on her. "I hear you're single. I'm happy to volunteer my services as your rebound guy."

Tatum looked at Dean, stunned. Was he serious? Dean had always been the hot guy, the ladies' man with the biting humor and the restless spirit. While there was no doubting he was nice to look at, he was—and always would be—Lucy's annoying brother.

Jared nudged his brother. "Seriously subtle, bro."

"Wow, Dean, just wow," Lucy said, shaking her head.

"Pissed I beat you to it?" Dean asked Jared, ignoring Lucy altogether. He grinned at Tatum. "Think about it, Tatum, if you're looking for a way to get back in the game—" He pointed at himself, cocking an eyebrow. "I'm just saying—"

"I think we all get what you're saying," Spencer barked. "But if we want to get the house ready for tonight, you'll have to hold off on your *sweet-talking* for now."

Tatum glanced at Spencer, taking in the tightness of his jaw and the slight narrowing of his eyes. What was surprising was just how much she liked his irritation over Dean's flirting.

While the others finished off their coffee, she ran back to her room to get her glove liners. It was cold and she wasn't as used to it as they were. If she was going to be any help she'd need—

She turned to find Spencer filling the doorway. "Spencer?" The way he was looking at her…it was hard to breathe.

She found herself pressed against the wall, his lips parting hers, his tongue seeking entrance and his hands holding her face. Her fingers threaded through his thick hair, pulling his head down to hers. There was nothing gentle about his touch or his kiss. It was possessive— claiming her, making her quiver and ache.

He pulled back, his eyes searching hers before he left her panting against the wall. She stood, trying to calm the frantic beating of her heart, as she heard the door open and close.

She was still pulling herself together when Lucy poked her head into her room.

"He leave you all hot and bothered?" Lucy asked. "'Cause he looks like a ticking time bomb. I thought you two would have, you know, done the deed by now."

Tatum felt the heat in her cheeks as she tugged on her glove liners.

Lucy giggled.

"We should go help," Tatum said, unable to stop the smile on her face.

Even with the glove liners, Tatum's fingers went from tingling to numb. The others had no problem wrapping the large tree in white lights. She and Lucy hung all the wood-chip angels, adjusting the lights so the whole tree was illuminated. When the only thing left was the star for the top, Jared and Dean held the ladder while Spencer teetered on the top step.

"Be careful, Spencer," she called up to him, wincing as he balanced on one foot to place the star.

"Will do." His voice reached her.

"Some things never change." Jared chuckled.

Jared was right. On the surface, it all felt very familiar. Except it was so very different now. She and Spencer had been young and crazy in love—strong and deep. Well, it had been for her. They weren't in love—how could they be? They didn't know each other anymore, not really.

This wasn't about love; this was about want. And she wanted Spencer more than she'd ever wanted…anything. She wasn't going to spend hours wondering about his thoughts or feelings. She was going to spend hours exploring his body and her sexuality. This *was* different.

Maybe it was reckless to invite Spencer into her bed when there was still such a strong connection between them. Maybe it was a mistake. Maybe she'd regret it... later. Right now, the thought of touching him, kissing him—having his hands on her—was all that mattered. Her body needed him in a way she didn't fully understand.

"Looks great." Mrs. Ryan joined them, gripping a large pot. "I made mulled cider, to help chase away the chill."

"Smells good," Dean said.

"Thanks, Auntie," Lucy joined in.

"Thank you so much, Mrs. Ryan. I know I'm freezing, so this will definitely help," Tatum agreed, ready to get inside. "It will go great with the stew I made."

"You go on in," Spencer called down. "We'll finish up out here."

"I'll carry it," Tatum offered, taking the large pot from Mrs. Ryan and heading up the path.

"I'll be in, in just a minute," Mrs. Ryan offered, making the three men groan. "Oh, shush, I only have a few ideas."

Lucy hooked arms with Tatum and headed inside.

"The cider was totally a ploy." Lucy laughed. "It's hard to argue with her when she's bringing you something to eat or drink. She'll probably have them out there another hour."

Tatum glanced back at the group, the three men stooping to hear whatever Mrs. Ryan was telling them. "Smart woman."

Lucy nodded. "Don't get me wrong, she loves to take care of people too. Especially her family."

The word *family* had become somewhat bittersweet to Tatum in the last few months. Most people took their loved ones for granted. But knowing she didn't have anyone was a very eye-opening experience. If and when she was ever lucky enough to find someone to love, she'd make sure they knew it every single day.

"I'm sorry about the divorce…about Brent being a cheating dickwad." Lucy's words ended her introspection. Her friend put the pot on the stove and hugged her. "God knows you've had more than your fair share of hurt."

She nodded again, hugging her friend. "Wanna know something funny? It was hard to accept he'd cheated on me. But when I figured out who it was with, I was devastated." She stepped back, pulling soup bowls from the cupboard. "Kendra is a couple of years younger than me, but not much. It's just…she and I weren't so different. I'd done everything he said he *wanted* to make him happy." She shook her head. "It turns out he really wanted a smart, career-minded woman—exactly what I had been when we married. Apparently Kendra is also terrific in bed." She shook her head. "Don't ask. Apparently Brent wasn't the first husband she tried to steal. Just the wealthiest."

"Miss him?" Lucy asked.

Tatum shook her head. "No. And I don't miss who I was when he was around." She smiled. "It's sort of liberating."

"And now you're free to explore other options—like Spencer."

She definitely wanted more exploring time with Spencer. Tatum pulled silverware from the drawers to set the table. "What about you? Are you seeing anyone?"

Lucy wrinkled her nose. "Nope. I'm not sure if it's the psychologist thing, having two brothers that happen to be cops, or the working for the police department, but guys seem a little…hesitant to date me."

Tatum looked at Lucy. She knew men looked at her friend—there was plenty to look at. Lucy was petite with killer curves and sassy pale blond curls. While they were both blonde, Lucy had a confidence Tatum had never felt. She remembered feeling invisible next to her in the halls of Greyson High School. Unless she was with Spencer. With Spencer, she'd felt special, beautiful and important.

"Their loss," Tatum murmured. "Maybe we need a girls' night? We can see what kind of prospects are out there."

"Maybe." Lucy shrugged. "Right now I'm happy to focus on my career."

They chatted a bit longer, laughing over some of Lucy's more memorable bad dates until Dean, Jared and Spencer joined them in the kitchen and sat at the table.

"Where's Mrs. Ryan?" Tatum asked, ladling the stew into bowls.

"She only brought the cider to soften us up," Jared explained.

"She wants us to redo the lights," Spencer said.

Tatum looked at them. "Are you serious?"

The three of them nodded.

"Too many holes." Spencer took the bowl she offered, smiling up at her. "I'll just add a few more strands and it'll be fine."

Once everyone had stew and bread, she sat beside Spencer. His hand rested on her thigh, making her jump. She saw his grin out of the corner of her eye.

"We're driving tonight, so you're on your own," Dean said between bites.

"Driving?" Tatum asked, trying not to think about Spencer's hand moving slowly up the inside of her thigh.

"The whole town gets officially lit up tonight," Jared

said, reaching for more bread. "Some of us have been volunteered to drive the judges through town."

"You volunteered?" Lucy's surprise was evident.

"Well, maybe we were told to. After that snake-in-his-drawer thing, the captain wasn't too happy, so…" Dean let the sentence hang there.

"You put a snake in your boss's desk?" Tatum asked, spoon halfway to her mouth.

"It was a grass snake." Jared shrugged.

"But he didn't think it was funny," Dean said.

"So they're driving tonight," Spencer finished.

"You didn't have anything to do with this, did you?" Tatum asked, arching a brow at Spencer.

He shook his head. "I tend to find ways to stay on the boss's good side, not his shit list."

They all laughed.

"Dean's a regular," Jared agreed.

Dean shrugged, his hazel gaze finding hers. "Guilty is as guilty does. And speaking of guilty, you have a chance to think over my little proposition?" He smiled.

Spencer's hand tightened on her thigh.

Lucy almost choked on her stew before sounding off. "First, yuck, she's my best friend and you're my brother. And, two, even if she did decide she wanted to take you up on your offer, do you really think she'd do so with an audience?"

Dean shrugged. "I'm all about full disclosure."

"How about we keep a little less disclosed," Spencer said, tearing into his bread and glaring at his cousin.

"Anyway…" Lucy glanced back and forth between them. "I'll be out in the cold, handing out maps for the light tour. I think I'd rather be driving around judges—at least you have heat."

Tatum shivered. "I couldn't do it." If she was this cold now, she could only imagine how frigid it would be when the sun went down. "I can bring you emergency hot chocolate?"

Lucy laughed. "That's okay. We set up in front of the fire station and they keep the hot chocolate and coffee coming. You can join me if you want? Didn't want you to be all alone tonight."

Tatum didn't miss the small smile on Lucy's face. Or the way Spencer's hand squeezed her thigh ever so slightly. "Oh, I have plenty to keep me busy. I haven't even started unpacking. Or cleaning out my bedroom. It seems strange for a divorced woman to be sleeping in a room with pom-poms."

Dean chuckled.

"Why not move into the master bedroom?" Lucy asked.

It made sense. It was her house now. But she wrinkled her nose at the thought. "I know I'm not ready to go through my mom's stuff. One thing at a time. Besides, I refuse to kick Spencer out until after the holidays. I'm not that heartless."

There was a slight silence, Dean and Jared exchanged an odd look, and Lucy was grinning. She didn't risk a look at Spencer.

Lucy nodded. "You've got time to make this place your own."

Her own. But did she really want to stay in Greyson? One of the reasons Gretchen, her college roommate, had invited her to San Diego for Christmas was to talk about an employment opportunity. Gretchen's family owned a finance and investment firm and, according to Gretchen, there was the *perfect* opening for Tatum.

Now was the time for trying new things, pushing her comfort boundaries and not passing up once-in-a-lifetime career opportunities. Even for great friends and amazing sex.

OVER THE YEARS, Spencer had wanted to punch Dean on more than one occasion. His cousin was good at finding his weakness and poking the shit out of it—until Spencer had enough. And right about now, Spencer had reached his limit with Dean's outrageous flirting and open admiration of Tatum.

She was sitting beside him, her scent pure distraction. It took everything he had not to run his fingers along the side of her neck, to bury his nose there and press a kiss to the hollow of her throat. He wanted to make her breath hitch and her hands tighten in his hair...

"Don't you think, Spencer?" Jared was asking.

He had absolutely no idea what Jared was talking about. But all four of them were looking at him, waiting for his answer. He had no choice. "About?"

Jared frowned at him. "New Year's?"

Nope. That didn't help at all. He waited, hoping like hell Jared would keep talking.

"Your brother's wedding?" Jared looked concerned.

Lucy went on. "According to Zach, we can stay after."

He glanced at Lucy, waiting. Why were they—

"Tatum's invited and I'm trying to convince her to come. If anyone needs some R & R, it's you, Tatum. Come on, we'll have the best time," Lucy pleaded.

He looked at Tatum. She was red-cheeked, clearly uncomfortable. Did she not want to go? Or...or was she thinking about the fact that their twelve days would be up by then? It might prove awkward to be in such close quarters after having such an intimate arrangement. But by then things wouldn't be as…urgent as they were now. Maybe. Possibly. If they were, having her there would be a good thing.

But beyond his hunger for her, he knew she was alone and no one should be alone during the holidays. "You should," he agreed.

"See," Lucy said, squeezing her arm.

"Let me think about it," Tatum said.

He glanced at the clock. It was almost two. He wanted to get the house done so he could take her on the lights tour. And then bring her back here and make her scream his name. He pushed back from the table, his abrupt movements making everyone jump. "Going back out," he said, standing.

Dean and Jared looked at each other, then him.

"I'm not done," Dean argued.

"Five more minutes isn't going to hurt a thing," Jared said.

"I didn't say you had to come with me," Spencer said. "Thanks for the stew, Tatum. It was delicious."

She smiled up at him, her green eyes bright. "You're welcome. Thank you for getting my—our—house up to judging standards."

Our house. Her words jolted him. "My pleasure," he said, winking at her before he hurried out of the kitchen. He liked what she'd said a little too much.

After finding more strands of white Christmas lights, he set about filling the holes his mother had found. And he tried his hardest not to let Dean and Jared lingering inside a hell of a lot longer than five minutes or the smile Dean wore when he did finally show up rub him the wrong way.

Ever since they were kids, Dean liked to get a rise out of him. This was no different.

"Damn, she's a good-looking woman," Dean said, taking some of the lights from him. "Why the hell did you dump her again?"

Spencer glared at his cousin.

"Gotta kill you, man. To see all that, back here, out of your reach." Dean sighed. "I feel for you."

Jared laughed.

Spencer continued to glare at Dean. "She take you up on your offer?"

Dean smiled. "Not yet."

"Then maybe she's not out of my reach," Spencer finished.

"Being roommates sure makes things cozy," Jared said, glancing at his brother.

They had no idea. "We'll see what happens," Spencer said.

"Right." Dean uncoiled some lights. "Or she might be over ancient history and want to try someone new. Like me."

"You can try." Spencer forced the words out, knowing his irritation was obvious but unable to do a damn thing about it.

But Spencer was the one staying tonight. He was the one who knew how to make her come apart at the seams and shatter in his arms. He knew how beautiful she looked when she climaxed. He turned back to the tree. But all he could think about was Tatum, the feel of her mouth on him...

"People are still talking about Wednesday night," Jared said. "Everyone's nervy."

Spencer hadn't given much thought to work. Clint

Taggart was bad news. It was about time the department had given him more than a warning or improvement plan. Spencer believed in backing his squad, but he didn't hold with putting the team in jeopardy. Which was exactly what Clint had done.

"You think Clint's going to follow through on his threat?" Dean asked.

Spencer shook his head. "If he wants to bring trouble to my door, I'll be ready and waiting."

Jared snorted. "Dumbass got himself in the situation, period. He doesn't know how to keep his mouth shut."

Which was true. Clint talked too much and too loudly. Which was a concern when you worked with undercover cops. As far as the department knew, no real damage had been done. Clint had drunk too much at a bar and mentioned a few names. Lucky for them, the bartender had been a source more than once and called Spencer. But, because Spencer had picked up Clint, Clint blamed Spencer for what happened next: Clint losing his job. And, before he left, Clint had threatened to beat the living daylights out of Spencer the next time their paths crossed.

"I'm not losing sleep over it," Spencer said.

"He was pissed. And pissed people do stupid things. Like sharing confidential information to get even." Jared looked at him.

Spencer paused, frowning. "I don't like Clint but I don't think he'd sell anyone on the team out."

Dean shrugged. "Guess we'll see."

They didn't talk much after that. Spencer couldn't shake the unease in the pit of his stomach. He took risks every day. He didn't need some asshole with a grudge getting him killed out of misplaced anger.

"Looks good to me," Jared said, standing back.

"She can't say there's a light shortage," Lucy said, as she walked outside to join them. "I've got to change and head to the fire station."

Spencer kept his impatience in check, trying not to think about Tatum waiting for him inside. His cousins helped him collect his tools and clean up the yard before they climbed into Jared's big black truck.

"You know she's over you, right?" Dean asked, grinning at him.

Spencer flipped him off, making both his cousins laugh as they drove away. He drew in a deep breath of cold air and made his way up the walkway. He stomped the snow off his boots on her porch and slipped inside. "Tatum?" Spencer called out. Unless she was waiting for him in the shower again. That would warm things up.

"Kitchen," she answered.

He headed into the kitchen. She had a large mixing bowl on the counter and a cookbook propped up. "What are you making?" he asked.

She turned, a smudge of flour on her nose. *"Pizzelle."*

"Oh, *pizzelle*," he said, then arched both brows. "What are *pizzelle*?"

She crossed the kitchen and threw her arms around his neck. "Yummy wafer cookies I have snowflake molds for. I thought I could make some for tomorrow night's fund-raiser?" She touched his nose. "Your nose is red." She was so pretty his heart thumped.

"It's cold out there," he said, pressing his hands to her cheeks.

She jumped, covering his hands with hers. "Your hands are freezing! Where are your gloves?"

"I took them off to mess with you." He winked.

"I like it when you mess with me," she answered.

His eyes narrowed, the corner of his mouth cocking up. "I like it too."

"Wanna help me make cookies?" she asked, swiping some cookie dough from the bowl and offering it to him on the tip of her finger.

He shook his head, sucking the dough off her finger and biting the tip. "I need to warm up."

She nodded, unzipping his coat and tugging it off. She draped it over the back of the chair before unwinding the black scarf from around his neck. She laid it atop the coat and pulled a chair out. "Sit."

He did, smiling as she turned and straddled his leg to pull his boot off. He had the most inviting view of her ass, hugged in tight jeans. When the second boot joined the first, he grabbed her around the waist and pulled her back onto his lap. His hands slid under the long black sweater she wore, the thrill of her flesh contracting beneath his fingers making him ache instantly.

His hands slid up, pausing when he encountered only smooth flesh. "You forgot your bra, Miss Buchanan."

"No, I didn't, Officer Ryan." She arched into his hands.

He groaned, burying his nose at the base of her neck. "You're soft as silk."

She shivered, the rapid thrum of her heart evident beneath his palm.

"You can't go out in public like this," he groaned as his fingers worked her nipples into hard peaks.

"I'm going out?" she asked, breathless.

"Can't miss the lights," he said, resting his forehead between her shoulder blades. He could wait. He didn't give a damn about the lights. But he wanted her to get out, to remember happier times and how good Greyson could be. "It's a tradition. I wanted to drive you."

She looked back over her shoulder. "I thought we were about sex. And sneaking around."

"Okay, forget the lights," he said, his hands cradling her breast more firmly. Not that he was going to let the subject drop altogether. Just for the next hour or so.

"Now I'll feel guilty. You should go." But she stood, faced him and straddled his lap. Her arms wrapped around his neck as she kissed him. He let her lead, let her lips part his and her tongue stroke the inside of his lip. He shivered, his arms winding around her waist and anchoring her in place.

"You want me to go?" he rasped.

Her green eyes sparkled as she stared at him. She nodded, then shook her head. "First, we need to warm you up," she purred, leaning forward to nip his earlobe.

He shivered as she sucked his earlobe into her mouth. She slipped from his hold and stood, pulling her shirt up and over her head and tossing it at him.

He caught it, soaking up the vision before him. "You're a beautiful woman."

"You don't have to say that," she said, an almost embarrassed tone to her voice.

He stood then, looking down at her. "It's the truth, Tatum. You're beautiful."

She blushed, tearing her gaze from his as she took his hand and tugged him toward the bedroom. The creamy line of her back demanded he touch her. They made it to the hall before he pressed her against the wall, running the tip of his nose along the base of her neck and the ridge of her shoulder blade. His hands cupped her breast as he trailed wet, hot kisses down her back. She sagged, leaning into the wall as he gripped her hips and ground against her. She arched into him, robbing his lungs of air.

"Dammit," he bit out, pulling her back against his chest and steering her into the bedroom.

She spun around, her parted lips latching on to his mouth. When his tongue slipped between her lips, he ground his hips against hers and bore her back onto the mattress.

"Spencer," she breathed.

His fingers were quick and deliberate, sending her clothing to the corners of her room. But the sight of her breasts quaking, her nipples tight peaks and her skin flushed shook him to the core. His hands were shaking as he fumbled with his clothing. By the time he'd climbed between her legs, he had no control left.

He pinned her hands over her head and pressed the tip of his rock-hard—

"Tatum?" a voice called out. A familiar male voice.

They froze.

"Left my phone."

"Is that Dean?" she whispered, the rosy hue of her skin draining as panic set in.

Yes, it was Dean.

And chances were the asshole had left his phone here on purpose so he could horn in on Tatum without an audience. Right now, so close to being wrapped in the heat of her body, he could give a rat's ass if his cousin found them like this. It would serve the smug-faced bastard right. "I'm guessing you didn't lock the door?" He smiled down at her, shifting his weight to remind her they'd been occupied.

She shook her head, breathless as she pushed against his chest. "Spencer," she hissed.

He wanted to argue but she was already sliding out from under him and pulling on her robe. "Stay here. I mean it," she whispered. Without looking back at him, she was gone. He flopped onto his back and stared at the ceiling, his heart hammering in his ears and his dick. The sight of her pom-poms made him smile.

TATUM TUGGED HER robe tight and walked into the living room. Dean stood, his cheeks red from the chill outside. When he saw her, his brows rose and his eyes widened. Yes, she was in her robe—with mussed hair when less than thirty minutes ago she'd been put together and civilized looking.

"You okay, Tatum?" He frowned as he looked down at her. "You look like you've been crying."

She felt her cheeks flame under his inspection. Crying was the last thing on her mind. "Oh? No…no, I'm fine."

"I know you've had a rough time of it," Dean said. "If I need to go kick some ass, I'm happy to do it."

"I appreciate the offer. But there's no one I'd want you to waste your time on." As long as Spencer stayed in bed. If he walked out…that might change.

His smile grew. "Then there's no one worth you wasting tears on, either."

His concern was sweet, even if the manly appreciation in his hazel gaze was a little overwhelming. All Dean was offering was a shoulder to cry on. While Spencer was lying in her bed…offering her his body. But nothing else. Not that she wanted anything else from him. From anyone, for that matter. She didn't. No complications, no expectations. No pain.

Losing Spencer all those years ago had taught her never to let go of her whole heart. Maybe that was why her divorce from Brent hadn't destroyed her. In a way, she should thank Spencer. But, with all the sex he was getting, she supposed she was.

"Tatum?" Dean asked, looking concerned.

She needed to snap out of it. "Sorry. You're right. No tears," she agreed.

"Good." Dean winked at her, making her giggle. "And if you need distracting, give me a call."

"I'll keep that in mind." She shook her head. "Did you find your phone?" she asked. She half expected Spencer to emerge any second—naked—just to stake a claim.

Dean held up his phone. "All good. I'm calling you now, so you'll have my number."

"Okay." Not that she'd call him. She and Spencer had a sex-only understanding. But Lucy was her best friend. No way she'd mess that up by dating Dean. Besides, as gorgeous as he was, she wasn't attracted to him like she was to Spencer. "Have fun tonight."

"See you later, Tatum," Dean said, before he left, pulling the door closed behind him.

Tatum counted to twenty before she locked the door and hurried back to her bedroom. She was amazed by how quickly her heart rate picked up. Her body seemed to rise, tighten, already sparking with the fire that gripped her moments before. Finding Spencer propped up on the pillows, the sheet resting low around his waist, was oil to her flame.

"He gone?" he asked, tossing a small heart-shaped pillow at her. "You two solve all the world problems or make your cookies while you were at it?"

She smiled. "I wasn't gone *that* long."

He cocked an eyebrow. And she leaned back against the wall, enjoying the view. His black hair was mussed, his jaw and chest dusted with a dark shadow. She could see the outline of one thigh beneath her sheet and the heavy length of his arousal. She swallowed, forcing her gaze back up to his. His blue eyes were blazing, and she stumbled over her next words. "Anticipation is a good thing."

"Not as good as being buried inside of you," he said, his voice rasping.

She exhaled slowly, a slight roar in her ears. He'd said that out loud, for her to hear. And from the look on his face, he meant it. Every muscle in her body tightened, clenching with pure need. "He's gone," she murmured.

"Come here," he said, not moving.

Something about the rigid line of his jaw made her pause. He wanted her. Badly. And it was empowering. She took her time crossing the room, aware of him watching her hands as she fiddled with the tie of her robe. "It's getting late," she said.

"No, it's not," he argued.

"You said the lights were a tradition." She stepped closer, transfixed by the way his body seemed ready to pounce.

"I'm in favor of making new traditions," he said, low and husky. "Believe me."

"Like making cookies?" she asked, teasing.

"Like getting you naked."

She swallowed, excitement coiling in her belly. She could do this. She could be sexy and provocative. His barely restrained hunger gave her all the encouragement she needed. She untied the sash of her robe and let the fabric slide from her fingers. She stood at the side of the bed, just out of his reach.

But she wanted him to touch her. She wanted him to

reach for her. So she shrugged out of the robe and waited. His eyes devoured her. Even without his hands on her, she felt the bold heat of his caress. She was so exposed like this. And in his eyes, she hoped, beautiful.

His hands fisted in the sheets at his side as she ran her hand along the column of her neck and across her shoulder. Her breathing picked up as her hand dipped lower, her fingertips sliding between her breasts and across her stomach.

The expression on his face hid nothing. He was a man on fire. For her. He tossed the sheet aside and slid to the edge of the bed, pulling her between his legs and pressing her tight against him. His mouth latched on to the tip of her breast, his lips and tongue stroking and licking until her nipple pebbled in his mouth.

Her fingers twined through his thick hair, holding him in place. When his teeth grazed her sensitized skin, she moaned. His lips moved along the swell of her breast and down her side. His tongue traveled around her hip. Somehow she ended up falling forward, her hands tangled in sheets. Spencer was behind her, exploring the plane of her back with his hands and mouth. He kissed the dip behind her knee. Nipped the curve of her ass. One long finger traced a slow path up the inside of her thigh.

With a growl, he clasped her hips in his hands and wrapped around her to suck her earlobe into his mouth. She felt him, the muscles of his chest against her back. The thick tip of his hard shaft against her, seeking entrance. She curved back, opening for him. And when he slid deep, she was done for. His hand slid across her stomach and between her legs. Calloused fingers worked their magic, the rough abrasion wreaking havoc on her tender, swollen flesh.

He shifted, standing at the bedside and pulling her back onto him. Strange noises spilled from her mouth, broken and low. Every time he moved, his hold tightened. It was the sweetest invasion, complete and absolute. Pushing her until she knew she'd split apart. And when his fingers found her again, she did. The desperate cry that tore from her startled her.

And then she was turning. Spencer's rhythm barely paused. From stomach to back, he was inside her, still relentless. Still wonderful. There was a slight sheen of sweat on his chest. His jaw was clenched tight. And he was staring down between them, watching as he moved in and out of her. His hand traveled down, his fingers stroking her again, and she was crying out her release again.

When his eyes met hers, he tensed, thrusting once, then again, before he climaxed. He slumped forward, pressing her into the mattress and blanketing her with his strength and warmth. She lay there gasping, her body still tingling with delightful twinges.

Spencer was equally breathless, hissing as he slipped from her to lie at her side.

She glanced his way to find him looking at her. "What?"

He shook his head, his gaze never leaving her face. It was the look on his face that made her heart slow…before tripping over itself in an unsteady rhythm when the corner of his mouth curved into a crooked grin. She wanted him to make her body hum with pleasure, but that was *all*. Her heart was off-limits. She frowned.

His grin grew. "How about we grab a couple of burgers and go check out the lights?"

"I've got things to do," she mumbled, deciding time alone, dressed and conversation focused were a bad idea.

He shook his head. "Well, you're going to have to feed me before I can *do* anything." His fingertips skated along her collarbone.

She smiled in spite of herself. "I wasn't talking about you." She shook her head. "I was talking about…"

He rolled over, rising up on one elbow. "About?"

"Unpacking."

"Unpacking?" he prodded. "What about tomorrow?"

"I have the women's auxiliary auction tomorrow night," she said, unable to ignore the curve of his bicep.

"What else?" he asked, his finger trailing between her breast and along her ribs.

"Nothing," she said, growing distracted by his teasing touch.

"So you can unpack tomorrow," he said, leaning forward to suck her nipple into his mouth. His tongue was wicked, erasing her argument completely. "And we can get those burgers and check out the lights. By then, I'll have enough energy to do whatever you want."

That was an offer she wasn't going to refuse.

6

SPENCER WAS CONTENT. Tatum sat in his truck, singing along with the Christmas carols on the radio and holding a steaming cup of hot chocolate in her hands. He drove five miles an hour down Cedar Bend Lane, uncaring that they were wedged, bumper to bumper, among the opening-night crowd. At the rate they were going, it would take an hour before they were done. And he couldn't be happier.

Not that their adventures in the bedroom an hour ago hadn't been amazing. They definitely were.

"Wow," she said, tapping the window at one especially lit-up home. "Check out those animatronics. Do you get extra points for that?"

"Depends on the judging committee. There was a big fallout a few years ago, the younger home owners wanting a voice on the judging committee and all."

"Sounds like serious stuff." She smiled, cocking her head as they drove past another house with a psychedelic lighting scheme. "I wouldn't give this one high marks... So what happened?"

"It was close, but the committee did have some turnover and there's a more *even* distribution of judges."

She glanced at him, sipping her hot chocolate. "I heard that."

"Heard what?"

She raised an eyebrow. "Sarcasm. What does 'even' mean?"

"Let's just say the whole age thing was fixed. But the overall mentality of the committee remains the same." He smiled at her. "I've never seen a first-time winner."

"Hmm." Tatum turned to look out the window. "That sounds like a challenge. If I'm still here next year, I'll have to pull out all the stops and see if I can steal one of those revered winner signs for my yard."

He heard the "if." He didn't like it. Not that now was the time to talk about what she meant. Not yet, anyway. As they pulled up to a large white column-fronted mansion with a double lot, he slowed. "Betty Brewer's grandmother still lives there."

She stared. "She's still alive?"

He chuckled, nodding. "Betty says her grandmother will live forever just to drive the rest of the city crazy."

"I remember her and her causes. The city-hall clock being a minute off. The need for school buses to have their brakes regularly oiled—to reduce noise pollution. Wasn't she one of the loudest voices in the fight to make this a dry county?"

"Damn happy that one didn't work out," he said. He loved the dimple in Tatum's left cheek. Loved the way her eyes creased when she smiled.

"I take it she hasn't mellowed with age, then?"

He shook his head. "Last city-council meeting she

wanted to discuss trash pickup times. Too early disrupts her sleep, too late and it's unsightly."

"She needs a hobby." Tatum laughed. "She and my mother got along famously—they played bridge together a couple of times a week. I remember visiting her house twice. The second time I bumped into an end table and knocked a tiny crystal lamb onto the floor. Its leg was broken. I felt terrible but Mrs. Brewer was *so* angry we had to leave. I wasn't allowed to come back after that and my butt was sore for days." There was no bitterness in Tatum's voice.

"How old were you?"

"Um…around six, I guess," she said, shrugging.

She might brush it aside, but the story reminded him of just how difficult Tatum's upbringing had been. Especially after her father had left. How many family dinners had been disrupted in their own home? His mother would sit there wincing as Mrs. Buchanan's shouts grew louder, staring at their father until he stood up, stomped across the street and warned Mrs. Buchanan that her behavior was crossing a line. Some nights, Tatum had come over to have dinner with them. And on one of those nights, he'd fallen completely in love with her.

"Does she win every year? Mrs. Brewer, I mean?" Tatum's question pulled him from the past.

He took a deep breath and eased his iron grip on the steering wheel. "Her house was disqualified from judging last year because she'd hired a decorating company."

"That's against the rules?" Tatum glanced his way as she took a sip of her hot chocolate.

"Only if it's not a local company."

"So I won't be disqualified? Since you and your cousins are from here?" she asked, turning her gaze back out the window. "I should do something for them—Jared and Dean, I mean. It was nice of them to lend a hand on their day off."

"Dean would love that," he muttered.

Tatum's shoulders were shaking. The sound of her giggle startled him. "So, it's okay for me to do something nice for Jared?"

"He's not trying to get you into bed."

She laughed then. "Dean might be trying to get me into bed but it's never going to happen. Lucy would kill me."

He almost rear-ended the car in front of them. "Lucy?"

"You don't sleep with your best friend's brother," Tatum said, watching him curiously.

He stared at her.

She was still giggling. "What?"

"Nothing," he growled. She was teasing him. He was acting like a child and he knew it. He had no right to be jealous—she'd laid out their arrangement clearly. No strings. No attachments. Just mind-blowing sex with an expiration date.

"What happened to Betty?" she asked.

"Betty?" he repeated. "Betty Brewer went off to college, married some guy and is living in Austin. She visits now and then with her kids."

"That's nice." This time there was an odd sound to her voice—high and tight.

Kids. God, he hadn't even thought about that. Did she and Brent have kids? Surely that would have come up by now. "Big commitment, having kids. Don't think I'll be ready for a while."

She glanced at him. "No?"

He shook his head.

"But you do want kids?" she asked.

He nodded. "Well, yeah, eventually."

"Be sure," she said, that tone edging her voice again.

"I'm sure."

"Just make sure you don't change your mind. Especially *after* you get married," she said.

He swallowed. No kids, then. Because Brent had changed his mind. He should be sorry for her but all he felt was relief. "You still want kids?" Tatum had always wanted a big family, one full of love and laughter—to make up for her childhood.

"Yes. I do." The longing in her voice made his heart hurt. She looked out the window, tapping on the glass. "*This* house is gorgeous. Oh, it's…magical."

Spencer made a point of keeping it light from then on. He wanted her to laugh, to smile and relax. That meant keeping talk of Brent and her mother to a minimum. When the drive was through and they were pulling up in front of the house, he could hardly wait to get her inside.

Tatum turned to face him. "I had fun tonight. Thanks."

He smiled. "Good."

"I'll see you tomorrow? At the women's auxiliary fund-raiser?" she asked, her hand falling to the door handle.

He tried not to let his disappointment show as he nodded. He'd envisioned a long night in her bed. How the hell was he supposed to *sleep* under the same roof?

She opened the door and slid from the truck. "Then I'll say good-night now." She slammed the door and headed inside before he'd turned the truck off.

Spencer sat there, staring at the front door. Maybe he should take a drive, clear his head, get a beer—anything to help him forget he was going to bed—alone.

TATUM STARED OUT the front window. She saw him sitting in his truck, looking at the house. Beyond the steady stream of headlights and the happy sparkle of her Christmas lights, he was there. Waiting.

She was testing him and she knew it. She'd sent him away and he was listening to her. Even if she hadn't really wanted to stay away, not really. What was she doing?

She crept closer to the window, watching him run a hand over his face, shake his head and back the truck out of the driveway. He headed down the road, his brake lights glowing red before he turned right.

"Fine," she gasped. "Good. Time to bake anyway."

She changed into some thermal leggings and a large sweatshirt, the feel of her own fingertips on her skin making her pause. Her fingers felt soft, not rough like Spencer's. She tugged her hair into a ponytail, irritated, and headed into the kitchen. She would not spend the rest of the evening pining for Spencer. Nope. She was going to do something…that wasn't Spencer. She smiled, blasted some Christmas carols and set to work.

She could make something else tempting to offer up at the bake sale tomorrow night. But what? Something about baking, which Brent approved of only when they were entertaining, brought out her rebellious side. She'd whipped up a batch of gingerbread, two blackberry-cranberry pies, some fudge, and finished two dozen *pizzelle* when her phone started ringing.

"Hello?" she asked.

"You up?" Spencer asked.

She smiled, running a finger around the inside of a bowl. "Clearly. It's a little late for a phone call."

"I knew I wouldn't sleep." His voice was gruff.

"Why?"

"Thinking about you."

She swallowed, walking from the kitchen into the front room. She glanced out the window. His truck sat there. "You're sitting in the dark?" She giggled. "Are you trying to have phone sex with me?" There was no way she could do that. It was too…odd. Listening to him telling her what he'd do to her. She felt incredibly warm. She'd touch herself and imagine it was him. Could she do that? Could she let the sound of his voice guide her until she—

"No."

She drew in a deep breath, willing her heart to return to a more sedate pace. "Oh."

He chuckled. "Don't sound so disappointed."

"Who said I was disappointed?" she lied. She'd rather he dragged his butt inside and had actual sex with her. "I'm tired. I'm going to bed."

"Tired meaning you'll be naked in bed waiting for me?" He paused. "Or tired meaning I'll see you tomorrow?"

She waited, knowing what she'd say but not wanting it to be too easy for him. *Oh, to hell with it.* "I'll see you in five minutes."

She ran to the bathroom, brushed her teeth, tossed her clothes on the floor and slipped the rubber band from her hair. She was running to her bed when she heard the door open. She squealed, hopping into the bed and burrowing beneath the covers. "That wasn't five minutes," she called out.

He was smiling when he entered the bedroom. "*I* never said five minutes." He started shrugging out of his clothes.

She slid to the edge of the bed, the quilts tangled about

her. Her fingers traced a long scar that curved around his side. "What happened here?"

He kicked his pants aside. "A knife. Two guys fighting over a woman in a bar. First week on the job. I was so green. And this is what happened. A tetanus shot and twenty-two stitches."

"Ouch." She looked up at him, catching another white line along his shoulder. "And here?"

He glanced at it. "A broken bottle. Woman didn't like me breaking up a fight. I didn't think she had it in her. Guess I was wrong. Eleven stitches and a staph infection."

She winced. "The one under your jaw?" she asked.

He traced the scar. "My brother Russ." He smiled. "According to him, I'd been in the swing too long."

Russ. She saw the flash of pain on Spencer's face and pressed a kiss on his tattoo. "What happened to him?" she asked, looking up at him.

He shook his head. "I can't. Not now."

She nodded, covering his tattoo in slow, openmouthed kisses.

He dropped his boxers.

And she stared at the rest of him. She couldn't seem to pull enough air into her lungs.

He stooped, pressing his open mouth to hers. In seconds, the quilts were gone and she was wrapped in nothing but Spencer. His arms, his lips and his tongue. She tugged him closer, running her fingers along his tapered waist and the clenched curve of his buttocks. He was man—muscle and power—and she wanted him. She parted her legs, panting, and arched into him.

"Impatient?" he rasped, his jaw tight.

She nodded. *Impatient* was an understatement. She'd been wanting him since she'd climbed out of his truck. Even making pie and gingerbread, she wanted him. So, so bad. "You weren't supposed to leave." Her words were bracing, too needy. She didn't like it.

His eyes searched hers, the tightening of his features unnerving her. "I won't."

God, she hated how much she loved the sound of that.

He thrust forward, filling her, joining them. His groan sent a thrill down her spine, forcing her nipples into tight peaks. When he moved, she knew it wouldn't take long to climax.

But he moved slowly, taking his time with her. There was a tenderness about him that made her nervous. She wasn't sure why he insisted on looking at her, why he whispered her name when she'd close her eyes or bury her face in her pillow. He seemed intent on…connecting.

His hand cupped her cheek, tilting her face and pinning her in place. She couldn't look away, couldn't fight the way his blue eyes claimed her. He cupped her breast, caressing her nipple and forcing her into pure pleasure. His steady, deep, rhythm had her falling. Her body contracted, her cry spilled out into the room, but all she could see was him. His face crumpled, hardening as he gave up the control he'd been exerting. He stiffened, fusing them together as he throbbed with his release. He kissed her, his groan shaking her to the core.

He rolled them, pulling her on top of him—crushing her in his thick arms.

Her body was humming, pleased and relaxed. But her eyes were burning with tears… Which was the last thing she needed. Spencer didn't need to see her that way. Emotional. Vulnerable. *Dammit*... It wasn't fair. She'd kept herself together when most people would have fallen apart. So why now?

Because I'm alone. Her heart thudded. Even now, wrapped in Spencer's arms, she was alone.

"You good?" His voice was low. His hands stroked down the length of her back, over and over.

She nodded, her tongue too thick to speak. She was not going to cry. Being alone wasn't a bad thing. She needed to stand on her own two feet—to figure out what she wanted.

He hugged her, sighing. "Sorry if I interrupted your baking."

She shook her head, swallowing the lump in her throat.

"Smells amazing," he murmured, his fingers combing through her hair.

She closed her eyes, absorbing his touch. Maybe that was the problem. Sex was one thing—affection was another. She pushed off of him, pulling the quilts up.

"Cold?" he asked.

She nodded, refusing to face him. "Tired," she murmured, flopping down on her side, her back to him.

He curved around her, his arm holding her against him. She sniffed as quietly as possible, wishing she was strong enough to move his arm and send him away. But she wasn't. She wanted him to hold her. She wanted him to press kisses against her temple, like he did now. She wanted him to stay. Which was a very big problem.

She lay there, listening to his breathing even out and his body go limp. There was far too much comfort in the weight of his arm and the whisper of his breath against her ear. What would happen when this was over and she was in a big, empty bed—aching for what she now knew existed? Before she could only imagine. Now she knew. How could she ever go back to Chris and his batteries?

7

"You're taking all of this?" Lucy asked, eyeing the double-stacked cake plate and Tupperware container full of her *pizzelle*.

"Too much temptation sitting around." Tatum smiled. "Tonight is the whole reason I made them."

"Spencer let you out of bed long enough to cook? That's considerate," Lucy teased.

Tatum laughed. "We're not that bad." Which wasn't true. Every time he was in the same room she wanted to touch him. And touching him quickly turned into more... *serious* touching.

Lucy snorted. "Whatever. Are you two really trying to keep this thing a secret?"

Tatum glanced at her friend. "This thing?"

"Tatum, there's obviously something going on between you two."

"It's called sex," Tatum argued. "*Nothing* else." She had to keep reminding herself of that. Waking up to him, his tongue stroking between her legs and his fingers sliding deep, had been the perfect way to start the day. The hot coffee and kiss before he left for work had been pretty damn wonderful too.

But after, when she sat in her bed, alone and cold, her melancholy returned. She almost gave in to it. Why not sob into her pillows? Wail a little? But she couldn't do it. It was too much like…giving in. Instead of thinking about what might happen after, she needed to enjoy every second of the before—the now. She'd crushed her pillow to her chest, immediately distracted by Spencer's scent clinging to the cotton pillowcase. She hugged it, breathing him in until she was smiling, and leaped from the bed. A cup of coffee and a long, hot shower had her perking up. So did putting on something pretty. When Lucy arrived with tea and some yummy little finger sandwiches and cakes, Tatum was feeling downright optimistic and full of enthusiasm.

"It's nice to have someone to hang out with," Lucy said, sipping her tea.

"Especially like this." Tatum grinned. "I feel like we should be wearing fancy hats and using my grandmother's china."

"Next time, definitely." Lucy grinned. "You going to be okay with Spencer going up for auction?"

Tatum frowned. "For auction?"

"You can buy one of our first responders for work around the house or something."

"Something?" Tatum asked.

"Last year a bunch of the elementary teachers put their money in to get a fireman to visit the school. Of course the whole station got into it. They spent the day there, making copies, playing with the kids, showing off the fire engine."

"And the money goes for?" Tatum asked.

"It's split. Half goes into the library and its literacy programming. The other half goes to the youth soccer association here. You know what a big organization it is here. They make sure there are scholarships and equipment, field repairs and referees for the games—that sort of thing."

Tatum nodded. Growing up, everyone had played soccer in Greyson. "So improving young minds and young bodies. Sounds like something that's easy to support. I'm sure he'll bring in a lot of money."

"Uh-huh." Lucy smirked.

She sipped her tea, then set it on the table. "How awkward is this going to be?"

"Very," Lucy said. "You're back. After…well, you know. People will be watching you two. And wondering."

Tatum stared into her tea. She did know. She could remember every horrible word he'd said, the horrified looks on the faces of her friends and classmates—

"Tatum, don't go there," Lucy said. "You don't know… He…" She shook her head, sat back in her chair and sighed. "He has regrets. Big regrets."

Tatum jumped up, busying herself with tidying the kitchen. "The past is in the past." She shot Lucy a smile. "I'm not stupid enough to let myself fall in love like that ever again. It wasn't healthy to be so connected with a person." She shrugged. "All I want is great sex."

Lucy looked doubtful.

"It's totally great sex," Tatum assured her.

"I don't want to know," Lucy laughed. "I just want you to be happy. Both of you. And I know he hasn't been really happy since you left."

Lucy's words bothered her. Surely that wasn't true.

Too many years had passed. She wanted him to be happy—even if it wasn't with her.

Tatum waved a hand at the containers of treats. "Let's load this up and see if your aunt needs any help."

"She and Spencer are probably already there," Lucy said. "Aunt Imogene is on pretty much every board in Greyson, so she's there in some official capacity or other."

They loaded Tatum's baked goods into her backseat. Lucy slid her sheet cake in and sighed, hands on hips. "You're making me look bad."

Tatum laughed as they climbed into her little beige SUV and headed to the other side of town. She drove slowly, the ice making her tires slip more than once. But going slow had other advantages. For one, she could enjoy every dazzling holiday display. For another, she could prepare for the night.

There wasn't much appeal in being surrounded by her past—especially the painful parts. But confronting them, making peace, was the only way to move on. And since she was sleeping with the person who'd actually hurt her, she figured handling the ones who'd simply watched the whole humiliating event wouldn't be too hard.

"Looks packed," Lucy said as they parked. "Ready? You certainly dressed to make an impression."

Tatum glanced at her red dress. It was modest. A sweetheart neckline, fitted sleeves and a full skirt. Lucy was wearing slacks. "Is it too much? I thought I was being festive."

"It's not too much. I just mean you're going to make tonight hard on Spencer." Lucy giggled as she climbed out of the SUV.

Tatum buttoned up her long black coat, collected her baked goods and followed Lucy up the bricked path to the large door of the Auxiliary Hall. Christmas music poured out the front door, mixed with jingle bells and laughter.

"Sounds like the party's already in full swing," Lucy said as they walked inside.

Tatum followed, placing her desserts on one of the long covered buffet tables that lined the hall. She tried not to make eye contact with anyone, tried not to let her nerves take root. But she couldn't exactly be antisocial at a social event.

"Can I take your coats?" Jared asked.

"Thanks." Lucy shrugged out of hers.

"Tatum?" he asked.

"Thank you." She slipped hers off and laid it over his arm.

He grinned, shaking his head. "Dean and Spencer are already at it, so you know."

"At it?" she repeated, cocking a brow.

"Arguing. Over you." Jared chuckled as he walked off.

She barely had time to process Jared's comment before Lucy clapped her hands over her mouth, a strangled giggle spilling through her fingers.

Tatum grabbed her arm, following Lucy's gaze. "Oh my God," she said before bursting into laughter.

Something about a man in an ugly Christmas sweater was funny. But seeing two really manly men in skintight pom-pom-covered sweaters—Spencer's was rigged with blinking lights—was beyond hilarious.

"Ugly Christmas sweater competition," Dean explained. His navy blue sweater sported two of the scariest elves Tatum had ever seen. Their huge yellow button eyes, arched brows and creepy grins were certain to give kids nightmares. The fact that they were peeking around a sequined

Christmas tree with pointy ice crystal ornaments only added to the whole disconcertingly ominous picture.

"You're going to make kids afraid of Santa's helpers," Lucy said, smacking her brother. "Parents will be investing in therapy instead of building blocks."

"What do you think?" Dean asked Tatum, pointing at his sweater.

Tatum grimaced. "I'm sort of creeped out."

Dean laughed.

"Runner-up," Spencer said. "But I'll give you an A for effort."

Tatum took in Spencer's sweater. Dark green with wide red stitching at the collar and cuffs, a googly-eyed reindeer head smiled at her. Not only did the deer's red nose glow brightly, but its antlers were decorated with pom-pom ornaments and lights that blinked rapidly. And when he turned around, the reindeer's rear end was visible. Its white tail swayed side to side, like a dog when it's happy.

"Nailed it," Spencer said.

Tatum dissolved into laughter again.

"You haven't seen Zach yet," Lucy argued. "Now that he's got Bianca's help, he might just give you a run for your money."

Spencer waved her words aside, his attention shifting to Tatum—a little too obviously for Tatum's liking. If he kept looking at her like that, people would know there was something going on between them. It didn't help that every time he looked at her like that, she immediately started thinking about what was going on between them. How incredible he was with his hands. And his mouth. His amazing rock-hard body. If she kept blushing, she'd be giving the whole town something to talk about.

"Where's your sweater?" Dean asked.

"Didn't get the memo," Tatum said, tearing her gaze from Spencer's. "Besides, you two… I can't compete with…*this*."

"Damn straight," Dean agreed.

Tatum tried not to let the sea of faces distract her. She recognized quite a few, but there was no animosity. Maybe a little open staring. If she could relax a little, she might find she was among friends. After years of self-doubt and second-guessing, she needed to stop looking for reasons to let her insecurity rise up to gnaw at her insides.

"You look beautiful," Spencer whispered.

When he'd made his way to her side, she wasn't sure. But his heat—his scent—was pure distraction. The kind she didn't want right now.

"You shouldn't look at me like…that." She glanced up at him.

His smile was too damn gorgeous, his blue eyes searching hers. "Like what?"

She blew out a deep breath, flushing beneath the weight of his gaze. "Like…that."

"Like I've seen you naked?" His voice was low—a tingle-inducing growl.

"Spencer," she hissed, her lungs emptying.

But Spencer was looking beyond her then, a very different smile on his face. She studied him, yearning for the affection and pleasure on his face. Not that she wanted him to look at her that way. No. But the idea of *someone* looking at her like that, someday, held a very definite appeal. She knew without looking that his brothers had arrived. His brothers, their wives…his family.

She forced her attention elsewhere. How much time had she spent staring at Spencer Ryan while she was in

Greyson? A lot. Too much. And even though his sweater was something of an attention grabber, she should not be staring at him right now. Not here, surrounded by people who'd last seen her sobbing hysterically because of him. The sharp twist of her stomach made her move away from Spencer and toward the table covered in baked goods.

"Can I help?" she asked Mrs. Ryan.

"Oh, Tatum, don't you look lovely?" She paused, then said, "Yes, dear, thank you." Mrs. Ryan patted her cheek. "If you don't mind uncovering those wedding cookies… and shifting that tray from the table's edge."

Tatum did, straightening the other items for sale.

"Drink?" Dean arrived, offering her a glass of white wine. "You look like a Christmas present. All ready to be unwrapped."

She snorted her wine.

He laughed, handing her a napkin. "Sorry."

She shook her head, patting her chin and mouth. "I'm not really sure how to respond to that. Thank you?"

He nodded, toasting her with his glass.

"Stop being sleazy, Dean." Lucy grabbed her arm, tugging her across the room to the newest arrival. "Come meet Cady and Bianca."

"Cady, Bianca, this is Tatum." Lucy made the introductions.

"I've heard so much about you," Bianca said, hugging her. "You're lovely."

Cady exchanged a quick smile with Bianca, her large eyes sweeping Tatum from head to foot. "It's nice to meet you." She nudged Patton.

Patton's hug was awkward and brief. "Welcome back, Tatum."

"Thanks, Patton."

"Hey, Tatum," Zach said, hugging her. "Glad you're home."

"It's nice to be back," Tatum said. "Congratulations to both of you. Well, all of you." She ignored the hollow ache in her stomach at the clear adoration both Zach and Patton had for their partners.

"Oh, hell no." Zach's surprised laughter drew all eyes. "You didn't?"

Spencer was behind her, grinning from ear to ear. His reindeer's nose blinked brightly.

"I told you I was going to own it this year," Spencer said. "Where's yours?"

Bianca sighed, rolling her eyes, as Zach shrugged out of his coat. He looked like he was wearing a Christmas tree, complete with needles, tinsel, ornaments and, yes, lights.

"That can't be comfortable," Spencer said.

"As long as I win," Zach said, draping an arm along Bianca's shoulders.

Bianca leaned away. "You're poking me." She giggled. "And making me itch."

"Sorry, babe." Zach took her hand in his. "Way to sport the evil possessed elves there, coz."

Everyone laughed then.

It was good, to be included—to laugh. There was an easy camaraderie among the men that managed to include the rest of them. And while Tatum tried to keep her distance from Spencer and Dean, Lucy made sure to stick to her side.

Somehow having a wingman made her reintroduction to Greyson easier.

When the dessert auction was done and the dancing was under way, Tatum helped the other women tidying up the kitchen. How her profession became the focus of conversation, she wasn't sure. But the three of them were spouting off all sorts of options.

"I think you should open your own office," Lucy was saying. "You've got the qualifications. I know a lot of women would welcome working with someone other than George Welch."

"Would you handle small business accounts?" Bianca asked.

"Yes," Tatum said. "I could—"

"Then I would hire you," Bianca cut in. "My cousin Celeste and I. That leaves more time for her to bake fancy tea cakes and for me to make the perfect floral arrangements for special occasions. We'd love to hand over our books to you. And I like the idea of women supporting women. A professional sisterhood, if you will."

"See," Lucy said, stacking up Tupperware dishes and covered cake plates.

"It's an idea," Tatum agreed.

"What other options do you have?" Cady was sitting on the counter, her shoes on the floor. "What's your plan?"

"Cady's all about a plan," Bianca murmured.

"What's wrong with planning?" Cady asked.

"I don't have one." Tatum shrugged. "Not yet. Only one real job possibility, in California."

"California?" Lucy asked, pausing.

Why were the three of them looking at her like that? "Yes. San Diego."

"San Diego is so expensive," Cady said.

"And there are earthquakes," Bianca joined in.

"It is a little far away." Lucy forced a smile.

Tatum glanced at each of them, surprised by their immediate objections. "Maybe the job will pay really well. And, yes, there are earthquakes occasionally, but there are tornadoes here. It might be a trek, but that's why there are airplanes. San Diego would be a great place to visit."

"Yes, of course." Lucy's quick response was forced.

And as the others made their way back to the table the Ryans were occupying, Tatum lingered by the refreshments. While she appreciated Lucy's determination to keep her involved, she didn't want to intrude.

Intrude. She heard Spencer's voice and glanced his way.

He was smiling at her, a brow cocked, as if he knew what she was thinking.

Her eyes narrowed and she crossed her arms over her chest, staying put.

He placed his beer on the table and stood, making his way to her—sending a rush of pure delight through her.

"Dance?" he asked.

She shook her head. That would be a very bad idea.

"I can behave."

"Maybe I can't." She looked at his mouth.

She was rewarded with the jump of his jaw muscle. "I say we make this evening more interesting."

She shook her head again.

"Me or Dean," Spencer said. "He's coming this way."

"Fine," she said, letting him lead her onto the dance floor. Tatum grinned at the blinking reindeer nose before he held her in a loose embrace.

"I'd hold you closer, but I wouldn't want to short out," he said.

She giggled, gasping as he spun her around. She had no idea he could dance. High school dances had been an excuse to hop around or slow dance, nothing like this.

But he knew what he was doing. While she was hanging on and trying to keep up.

"Take up ballroom dancing?" she asked, stunned.

"A mom-required event." His gaze fell to her mouth. "Just hold on to me."

Her insides quivered. "I am."

The song blurred into another, a slow rendition of "What Child Is This?" It was a perfect slow dance song, the perfect excuse for him to pull her closer. "You might short out," she murmured, all too aware of the effect his nearness was having on her. And she knew what she was doing to him too.

A quick assessment told her there weren't many couples on the dance floor.

"It's fine." His voice was rough, pulling her eyes back to him.

"No, it's not," she whispered even as his fingers splayed across her back, his palm pulling her close.

"We're just dancing," he assured her.

She forced her gaze down, the flicker of his sweater lights making her grin. Maybe she was taking this a little too seriously. Maybe his response to her wasn't visible.

"I admit, I like holding you," he murmured softly. "You feel good."

"Your lightbulb is poking me in the stomach," she lied, adding, "It's hot." It wasn't, but she was getting there.

He eased his hold on her. "My lightbulb, huh?"

She giggled. "Yes, your lightbulb."

"It's been called a lot of things, but…"

It took her a while to stop laughing. By then the music was over and he was leading her to their table. Lucy squeezed over so they could share a chair.

"Almost sweater time," Jared said, pointing at Dean and Zach by the steps leading to the stage.

"Time to kick some butt." Spencer was all smiles as he headed to the stage.

She tried not to stare at his ass. Horrible sweater aside, his black trousers made up for it.

"I talked to the one real-estate office in town and a dentist, Dr. Maria Klein." Cady slid two cards across the table to her. "Here. They'd love to speak to you about becoming their accountant. And Mrs. Monroe." Cady touched Tatum's hand, then pointed out the black-haired matron. "She said she'd be happy to use you. She owns a shop on the main square selling…" She looked at Patton.

"Kitchen stuff." He shrugged.

"Which you should know, Cady dear, since the two of you should have registered there already. It went out in the invitations." Mrs. Ryan sighed. "You two."

Cady grinned at her future mother-in-law. "I'll drag him there tomorrow."

"Joy," Patton muttered.

"Come on, Aunt Imogene, be happy this is happening," Lucy said. "Patton was fine with Cady's idea of eloping."

Mrs. Ryan groaned and covered her face with both hands.

"One of the hotels Zach manages had a wedding cancel at the beginning of the month. Cady and Patton stepped in, making everyone happy." Bianca smiled.

Patton didn't look very happy, but Tatum didn't say a thing.

"You are coming?" Cady asked. "It's New Year's. In Aspen. At some swanky hotel. So you should come. Dance, laugh, have fun." She glanced at Spencer, then back at her.

It was hard to miss the other woman's message. But

by then, her time with Spencer would be up. Attending his brother's wedding, surrounded by family and close friends, would be beyond awkward.

"Come on, Tatum," Lucy whispered. "We can be roomies."

But she was saved by the static of the microphone and the emcee's announcement. "Good evening, ladies and gentlemen. We have our ugly sweater contest first. The winners of our silent auction. And then the big event, our bachelor auction."

SPENCER COULDN'T BREATHE. He was in serious trouble and he knew it. Watching her, every smile, every laugh… He wanted to take her hand so Dean would back the hell off. He wanted to take her hand so everyone knew she was spoken for. Even if she wasn't.

His hand tightened around his beer bottle.

Her long blond hair spilled over her shoulder as she leaned forward to listen to what Lucy was saying. Her neck arched, pale and graceful. He knew how that skin felt beneath his lips, how she tasted.

He took a swig of his beer.

"Congratulations," Patton said, sliding into the empty chair at his side. "A plastic trophy and a day helping Mrs. Graham around her house."

He glared at his brother. "Jealous?"

Patton shook his head, his crooked grin quick. "Hell no."

Spencer laughed. "How's the wedding thing going?"

It was Patton's turn to glare. "Don't go there." He paused. "She looks good."

Spencer knew who they were talking about. "She does."

"Cady likes her."

"What's not to like?" he asked.

Patton didn't say anything.

"What if I more than like her?" Spencer asked softly.

Patton smiled a real smile. "You always have."

The truth in his brother's words was freeing—and terrifying.

Patton cocked his head, meeting his brother's gaze. "If she can forgive you for what you did, you're probably the luckiest son of a bitch of all time."

Spencer nodded, taking another swig.

"You two talk?"

"No." Talking was the one thing they hadn't done. His gaze returned to her. She reached up, absentmindedly brushing her hair from her shoulder and resting her hand on the table. She'd painted her nails red...

Patton chuckled.

"What?" Spencer asked.

"Just wondering if I was that obvious?"

Spencer sighed, setting his beer bottle on the table. "You were. And you are."

Patton shrugged. "Cady's trying to get her to stay."

"To stay?" Spencer asked.

Patton looked at him, frowning. "Some job in San Diego?"

He knew she was going to visit a friend. But a job? A job in California—a job that would take her away. Again. He picked up his beer, draining the bottle. He had no right to ask her to stay. Hell, he didn't even know if he wanted her to stay.

Which was a lie. He knew.

"Spence?" Patton asked.

"Time for her to do what she wants." He smiled at his

brother, ignoring the cold, hard lump settling in the pit of his stomach. He did want her to do what she wanted. He'd just hoped it would be here.

It wasn't like he'd spent time envisioning a future for them. Even if he had, if he did, no one knew that but him. He wouldn't influence her again. Whatever choice she made would be hers this time.

8

SPENCER YAWNED, BEYOND tired as he steered his truck down the dark streets toward home. Nothing like working forty-eight hours straight. A long forty-eight hours. Between Clint's disappearance and a pop-up meth lab tip, he'd driven over most of the county and turned up nothing but an abandoned barn and cold trails. He'd busted two teens selling pot at a corner store but lost another in the park.

At least he hadn't spent much time at his desk. Nothing like sitting underneath humming fluorescent lights to make a man doze. Being up, out, adrenaline pumping, kept him sharp and focused.

He hadn't been slated for the shift, but when his co-worker's wife had gone into early labor, he'd volunteered to cover the man's shift. Unlike the vast majority of the Greyson force, he was single.

Had Tatum noticed he was gone? Missed him at all? He blew out a deep breath. Dammit, he'd thought about her a hell of a lot over the last forty-eight hours.

There'd been a time when she would have confided in him. Now he was learning about possible jobs in California. She was thinking about leaving? And he finds out through Patton. Through Cady. Someone Tatum had met that night knew more about her than he did.

He shouldn't be hurt. Or angry. So why was he? He'd agreed their relationship was purely physical. In her mind, there was no reason to tell him she might be moving on. At that point, she'd be done getting in touch with her sexual side. And done with him too, apparently.

But his heart was confused by the whole no-strings plan. Spending a little time away from her had been good. And bad. He'd done some thinking—about her. And, after so much sex, the last two days had been hell. And his body was aching to pick up where they'd left off.

He pulled into the driveway and turned off the engine, the heat escaping into the frigid night.

Two cars were parked along the curb. Lucy's and Bianca's. Meaning his plans for stripping her down would have to wait. Upside, he might get a few hours of sleep. He was whistling as he climbed the steps.

"You look like shit," Lucy said as he stepped inside.

"Thanks," he grumbled, his eyes sweeping the room. There was a board game on the floor and empty wineglasses. And Tatum was in pajamas, smiling at him. What would happen if he threw her over his shoulder and took her to bed? He was tempted to try. "Don't let me interrupt."

"You look tired," Tatum said. God, she was beautiful. "We'll keep it down."

He nodded. "Shower. Bed. Sleep." He saluted them and walked down the hall to his bedroom, smiling at the sound of their voices and their laughter before he closed the bedroom door.

He liked her pajamas. He liked the smile she wore for

him. He groaned, wiped a hand over his face and headed for the bathroom. He stood under the hot water until it ran cold, then stumbled into bed. The red numbers on his side-table clock told him it was nine. The garage light illuminated his room, casting an eerie white glow. But he was too tired to get up and close the blinds. He threw his arm over his eyes and passed out.

He woke to faint knocking. At two in the morning? He glanced at his phone. No calls. He was disoriented, exhaustion weighing him down. He opened the door to find Tatum in a silk robe.

"I've missed you," Tatum whispered.

He could be dreaming. She filled his dreams often enough. Maybe he was dreaming.

But then he was engulfed in her sweet softness and he didn't care. Her lips found his, her tongue slipping between his lips at the very moment she pressed her silk-covered curves against him. He groaned, grabbing her with both hands. In an instant, he was throbbing and ready.

Definitely not dreaming.

Her lips teased his throat, his shoulder, her tongue explored the hard contours of his chest—torturing his nipples and his patience. She slid down, the caress of silk on his bare skin incredibly erotic. When his boxers were around his ankles and her lips latched on to his rock-hard erection, he shuddered, leaning against the wall at his back.

He stared down, his fingers in her blond hair and tugging her back.

Her fingers continued to stroke him as her gaze locked with his. "Hi," she said, before bending forward to suck him deep into her mouth.

"Shit," he hissed, her hand cradling him as her tongue slipped around his length. Her lips were like velvet, hot, sucking, drawing him forward. In seconds, she had him on the edge.

He gripped her shoulders and pulled her up. His kiss wasn't gentle, his teeth and tongue showed her just how hungry he was for her. When he tried to ease his hold on her, she pressed closer, welcoming the invasion of his tongue. Her little gasps, the tight hold on his hair and rake of her nails on his neck, had him all but dragging her to the bed.

She wasn't wearing anything beneath her robe.

Her nipples were so hard he couldn't resist. Before she answered, he'd sucked the puckered flesh into his mouth, cupping the fullness of her breast with his hands.

She writhed, her long, toned legs parting as her hands sought some anchor.

He threaded her fingers with his, stretching her arms up over her head as he drove into her.

"Oh, God, Spencer…" Her moan was raw, desperate.

"Miss me?" he ground out, her tight heat challenging his control. He wanted her to miss this, his ownership of her. He wanted her body—and more.

"Yes," she rasped, breaking off as he powered into her again.

Long, slow strokes that filled her up and left him trembling.

Her fingers opened and closed, gripping his hands as his mouth pressed along the length of her neck. He nipped the flesh beneath her ear, drew her earlobe into his mouth and never broke the deep, hard rhythm he set.

"Spencer!" she cried out, her body beginning to shudder as she tightened convulsively around him. He watched, loving her climax—the total abandon in her release.

He held on, never breaking rhythm, never slowing. He hovered over her, his chest brushing again and again over the taut little peaks. His mouth returned to her breast, his tongue laving and flicking until she was gasping again.

His hands clasped her wrists, pinning her in place while giving him more leverage. "I could do this all night," he murmured.

She shook her head, already close to coming again. "Please…"

"Please what?" he asked.

"Touch me." Her voice shook. Even in the shadows of the room, he knew she was staring at him.

He released her hands. His fingers slipped between them, his thumb working over the throbbing nub between her legs. And just like that, she was burying her face in his pillow to scream.

He let go then, out of his mind as he thrust. When his orgasm hit him, he bit out a curse, long and loud—holding her hips steady.

He fell to her side, breathing as if his life depended on it. But once he'd left her, all the anger and frustration he'd held at bay came crashing down. "Why didn't you tell me about California?" he asked, still gasping.

"What?" she asked, equally breathless.

Shut up. "The job, in San Diego." He paused, turning on the bedside lamp. "You made it sound like a vacation."

She blinked, looking so damn adorable with her tangled hair and flushed cheeks that he almost dropped it. "I didn't think it mattered," she said, her brow creasing. "Or that you'd care."

He stared up at the ceiling, his heart thumping heavily.

"Spencer?" she asked.

He didn't say anything. What could he say? "I care." Which were probably the last words he should say.

The silence grew painful. But he couldn't take it back. It was the truth. He cared. He loved her. So damn much. He'd loved her his whole life. He closed his eyes, his hands fisting in the sheets.

She pulled the blanket up and over her but didn't say anything. He lay on his side, waiting. But when she did look at him, she broke his heart. Her green eyes were full of unshed tears and her lips were pressed flat. Even though she was stiffening, pulling away from him, he saw the flash of vulnerability—and reached for it. He rolled over her, keeping her close before she completely shut him out.

"Let me go, Spencer." Her voice trembled.

He brushed his nose against hers, staring down into her huge green eyes. "We need to talk."

"No, we don't," she argued softly.

He shook his head.

"No complications, remember?"

"Just sex?" he asked, an undeniable edge to his voice.

"Yes," she replied, nodding and blinking rapidly.

"Fine," he said, bending his head to kiss her. It wasn't fine. It hurt like hell. And pissed him off. Why wouldn't she let him apologize? Let him beg for another chance? Yes, he wanted her. He'd always want her, but that didn't change his feelings. So he poured his frustration, his pain and anger, into his kiss. He kissed her until her arms wrapped around his neck, until she rolled over him and straddled him.

When he slid home, he gripped her hips and held on. It took seconds for him to come undone, for her to find her release. But he held on to her long after they were done. If sex was what she wanted, he'd give it to her. Until he figured out how to change her mind—and he *would* figure out how to change her mind—sex was the only time she was his.

"CADY'S ALREADY GOT a client list for you," Lucy said, pulling up the strap on her plum evening dress.

"She's…something," Tatum said, grimacing at her reflection. "This one is a no."

"She's assertive. And bossy." Lucy's friend Celeste had joined them for shopping. "I can say that because I've known her for years but I love her anyway."

Tatum laughed. "I appreciate her interest. It's just surprising. She doesn't really know me. I could be a terrible accountant, bad with people…" She shrugged.

"She's very girl-power. She knows you've been through a painful divorce," Celeste said, almost apologetically.

Tatum smiled. "It's not a secret. I know I'm not the last woman to lose her man to another woman."

"That's pretty much all it takes for Cady. You've been wronged, by a man, she's going to help out."

Tatum accepted what Bianca said, but there was one nagging suspicion. "So it's not to keep me here? I sort of get the feeling that she…all of you want me to stay here?"

"This *is* your home." Lucy sighed. "And, yes, I admit, I want you to stay," Lucy said. "It's hard being the only girl in a family of boys."

"You should marry one of her brothers, Tatum." Celeste was all smiles. "They're both incredibly good-looking."

Lucy shook her head emphatically.

"They are good-looking," Celeste argued.

"Couldn't do it. I grew up with them." Tatum reached for the next dress on the rack. "More brother than not.

Even if I've never had a brother. Jared used to put worms in my pudding. And Dean was always trying to look under my skirt or down my shirt. But he did punch a guy for me once." She laughed.

"I remember." Lucy grabbed Tatum's hand. "We were, what, twelve?"

Tatum nodded. "Twelve was such an awkward time. I got my braces and my boobs. This boy in my class was teasing me—"

"And Dean socked him in the face," Lucy finished, her face turning thoughtful. "Huh. I'd almost forgotten about that. I'm just not sure what he's trying to do. Piss off Spencer or get you to date him."

Tatum shook her head. "He's just being Dean. He's teasing." She thought about his rebound-guy offer and grinned. He wasn't serious.

"He and Spencer have had this competitive thing for-ever." Lucy sighed. "Boys."

"I'm confused. How is Spencer involved?" Celeste asked.

Somehow, he's always involved. But she didn't say any-thing. Her emotions were too raw at the moment. And she didn't know what to make of them. Or how to face them.

"Spencer and Tatum were pretty serious in high school," Lucy explained.

"A lifetime ago," Tatum murmured, the onslaught of conflicting emotions hurting her head. She let the light-weight material of the blue Grecian dress slide through her fingers, absentmindedly.

"High school romances," Celeste said. "First love. Oh, the memories."

"I never dated in high school." Lucy frowned. "Not high school boys, anyway."

While the others kept talking about past relationships and high school, she tried on the blue dress. Talking about either meant talking about Spencer. She was doing plenty of that already. Lucy had promised to take Celeste dress shopping for Cady and Patton's wedding and dragged her along too. And while Tatum wasn't sold on going to the wedding, she figured spending a day out was better than analyzing what had happened the night before. With Spencer.

"You look gorgeous," Lucy said with a sigh. "It just hugs in all the right places."

"Drop-dead gorgeous," Celeste agreed. "Unlike this." She spun around in a pea green jersey dress stretched taut over her sizable chest.

They all laughed.

She did feel pretty in the dress. And, whether or not she went to the wedding, it couldn't hurt to have something new in her closet. Memory-free. Especially when it made her feel like this. "I think I'll get it." She tugged her clothes back on. "I'm going to do a little Christmas shopping while you finish up."

She carried out her dress and wandered along the racks and aisles of holiday items. She hadn't meant to wander into the lingerie section, but that was where she ended up. And an especially sheer black lace number with a built-in push-up bra and matching lace thong caught her eye. That was undeniably sexy. And since she'd clearly established that they were all about the sex, this would be a perfectly acceptable purchase. She took it, strolling past the jewelry and accessories, her eyes drawn to a large variety of silk scarves on the back wall. Even though the saleslady had no idea what the four silk scarves were for as she packed them next to her sexy lingerie, Tatum couldn't help but blush. She was buying stuff to tie up her... Spencer.

She took her time, poking through shops along the square. She bought Lucy her favorite perfume, added a baking cookbook for Mrs. Ryan and picked a lovely set of embroidered sheets off Cady and Patton's bridal registry.

As she was coming out of the shop, she spied a candy shop across the street. If she remembered correctly, Spencer's favorite candies were jelly beans. The small ones with the superstrong flavor. Some of her favorite memories were of them eating jelly beans in the dark on her roof and tossing all of the buttered popcorn–flavored beans into the dark. She paused, so caught up in the past that she was *there*. His laugh. Her head pillowed on his shoulder. His kiss on her temple. He'd been smaller then, with fewer muscles, but his love had been as constant as the stars above her. She'd trusted him, them. They'd spent hours there on summer nights, talking, just hanging out together. He'd always held her hand, always. She could almost feel his hand on hers now.

I care.

What did that mean? Did she want to know? What if it meant opening up old wounds? She'd bled enough from the past.

Before there was the bad, there had been so much good. She'd let one week of hell—and a moment of utter humiliation—tarnish something that had helped her through so much. He'd been a pillar in her life, a support, something she'd clung to when her parents fell apart. When her grandparents died. Her mother. How many times had he rescued her, built her back up when her mother had torn her to shreds?

There'd been love and laughter too. With jelly beans

and tickle fights, and making out until they both needed to cool down. Maybe reliving that wouldn't be so bad? But reliving the good always led to the end. One day Spencer had been her world, the next he didn't love her anymore. She still didn't know why.

Maybe the why shouldn't matter anymore?

She made a beeline for the shop, purchasing a large bag of assorted flavors before heading back to the clothing store.

They had mani-pedis before Celeste headed to Tucker House to set up for the bridal shower, and Tatum and Lucy went back to Tatum's place to change. By unspoken agreement, their conversation steered clear of all things men and focused on career.

Lucy had been working as the police psychiatrist for a couple of years, working under a veteran psychologist she didn't always see eye to eye with.

"It's the old-boy network, you know? If he likes a guy, he's more likely to send them back out—even though there's no way in hell they should be on the streets." Lucy sighed, leaning forward to apply eyeliner in the large mirror hanging on the closet door.

"I'm sort of glad my career choice doesn't involve weaponry," Tatum teased. But she was serious. She'd lost so many people in her life, the idea of being surrounded by life-and-death situations on a daily basis held no appeal. Another reason not to get attached to Spencer. "Seriously, I respect what you do. I don't think I could."

Lucy shook her head. "Ditto. I could never work with my husband. If I had one." She giggled. "I only met Brent twice, but he seemed like a hard man to please."

"He was very opinionated. His way was always the right way. The work was no big deal, I know my stuff and I did my job. Honestly, we were better at being coworkers than a married couple. Especially in the bedroom."

Lucy's brows rose. "Do tell. Was he crooked?"

"He was small. He was a straight-missionary, lay-there-quietly and no-cuddling-after sort of guy."

Lucy frowned. "Well, that's just sad. But didn't you sleep with him before you were married?"

"He wanted to be traditional. I was fine with it. I thought it was sweet."

"My sex life sounds better than yours," Lucy offered.

"I thought you weren't seeing anyone?"

"I'm not," Lucy said. "Still better."

Tatum burst out laughing.

"I am sorry, Tatum. I know…" She paused. "I know Spencer hurt you. If he hadn't, I think you two would already be married."

"Probably," she agreed. The few times she'd let herself go there, it had been pretty idyllic. A dream versus a reality. "But that doesn't mean we'd be happy."

"Why wouldn't you be?" Lucy argued. "You were. So was he."

"If he'd been happy with me, he wouldn't have dumped me." She cleared her throat. "Not that I want a relationship right now—I don't. At all. But later, much, *much* later, I'm hoping that whole third-time's-a-charm thing applies to me."

Lucy hugged her. "Me too, Tatum. Me too."

At least Spencer hadn't made it awkward this morning. Okay, waking up to an empty bed was hard, but she hadn't had to worry about facing conversations or feelings, doubts or worries where Spencer was concerned.

Instead of overanalyzing things—again—she'd sat up and taken a look around what had been her parents' bedroom. Spencer, or someone, had done some major work in the space. The horrible wallpaper was gone. The shag carpet pulled up to reveal wood floors. It was lovely. As was the master bath.

Which made her wonder what the rest of the house could look like.

"Change of subject, but I've been thinking about the whole home-office thing—"

"You have?" Lucy interrupted.

"The house needs some work." Tatum nodded.

"If you and Spence decide to keep your hands off one another for a day, I'd be happy to come over and help you with the house."

"I was hoping you'd say that." Tatum smiled. "I've never really had the chance to make a space my own. I think it could be fun." And it would increase the house's resale value.

"Are we talking the whole house? Not just turning your bedroom into a fully functional office space?" Lucy's smile grew at Tatum's nod. "I'm so excited."

Tatum stood in the middle of her bedroom, staring at the lavender walls, the tacked-up pictures and remaining high school memorabilia. She'd started pulling things down and boxing them away but it was depressing as hell. An emotion she was trying to avoid.

"This room makes more sense as an office." Lucy opened the blinds on the two windows. "Behind this is an exterior door?" She tapped on the floor-to-ceiling bookshelf.

Tatum nodded. Her mother had it sealed from the outside, but surely that wouldn't be too big a fix? She could put in a stone path directly to the office so it was separate from the rest of the house. And the large windows offered a gorgeous view of a greenbelt. In a few months, the fields would be covered with vibrant bluebonnets, touches of red and yellow and pink.

Tatum said, "I can almost see it."

"That's the first step, then. Visualization is a solid step toward implementation." She giggled. "We need to go to the hardware store and look at paint samples too. I think a sleepover might be required. S'mores, wine, architecture magazines. Maybe a movie too?"

"I like it," Tatum replied. "Just promise me no chick flicks and I'm in."

Lucy nodded. "How about action flicks with shirtless hot guys?"

"Deal."

9

SPENCER SHIFTED THE large Crock-Pot he'd picked up for the happy couple and opened the door of Tucker House.

"You look wiped," Zach said, giving him a one-armed hug.

"Skeleton crew means extra hours," he said, hugging Bianca. "You look pretty."

Bianca smiled. "Thank you, Spencer."

"Where's the happy couple?" he asked, assessing the crowd. Chances were he could put in an appearance and sneak out. He needed sleep. He'd been called in to work and left Tatum sleeping, warm and soft in his bed. Leaving her was that much harder knowing he had five days before their twelve days were up.

Hell, he could sleep later.

"Library, I think," Bianca said.

He nodded, shifting the box again, and headed toward the library. The last year had been all about weddings and everything leading up to it. He was getting pretty damn comfortable with the B and B that housed many of their events.

The first person he saw was Patton. And he looked

like he could use a drink. Spencer deposited his gift on a table already stacked high with presents and went to the bar. But bumping into Tatum, having her fall into him, almost made him drop the two longnecks he was carrying.

"Sorry," she said, her hands resting on his chest.

His arms had wrapped around her, to stop her from falling to the floor. "Nice catching up with you."

She rolled her eyes, smiling broadly. "Was that a pun?"

He shrugged. "Maybe."

"It was pretty bad." She looked at his arms, still anchored around her waist. "I'm good."

He leaned forward. "The best," he whispered in her ear. He let go of her, but not before he'd felt the shiver that racked her.

Her eyes fastened on his, then on his mouth. *Good.*

He winked at her and headed toward his brother, hoping he looked cool, calm and unaffected by the brush of her curves and sweetness of her scent.

"Beer?" he asked Patton, offering him the bottle.

"Way to make an entrance." Patton took the beer and drank deeply.

"You look like you're having a great time, bro," Spencer retorted.

Cady looked at Patton and laughed. "You want to cut and run?"

"Only if you're coming with me," Patton said.

She took his hand in hers. "Nope. You're stuck right here. But I promise I'll make it up to you later."

"Hey, hey." Spencer made a show of covering his ears. "Little brother here."

Patton laughed.

Cady was looking at him, curiously. "So, little brother, I have a question for you."

"Here we go." Patton took another sip of his beer.

"Shoot," Spencer said, searching the crowd for any sign of Tatum.

"You love her?" Cady asked.

He looked at his almost sister-in-law. "Straight for the jugular, huh?"

"That's Cady," Patton murmured.

"And you adore me." Cady smiled up at her fiancé.

Patton nodded, looking at Cady in a way that made Spencer slightly uncomfortable. "I sure as hell do," he said in a gruff voice.

"I'd tell you to get a room, but..." Spencer teased.

Cady glared at him. "Patton says she's the one."

Patton groaned.

"He does?" Spencer glared at his brother. "Did he tell you I messed it up?"

She nodded. "You were pretty much the biggest asshole ever, from what I've gathered. But things like confessions and apologies make a difference. So does hearing 'I love you.'"

He swallowed. "She doesn't want a relationship."

Patton and Cady both looked at him.

"She's saying that because she's scared," Cady assured him. "Wouldn't you be? Both the men she committed to dumped her."

He didn't say anything.

"Is she what you want?" Patton asked.

He nodded.

"What are we talking about?" Zach joined them. "It looks serious."

"Your brother and Tatum," Cady offered.

"Okay." Zach nodded. "I need a drink."

Spencer laughed. "Conversation's over, don't worry."

He smiled at Patton and Cady. "Congrats, guys. I'm really happy for you. And I appreciate your concern."

He excused himself and wandered into the billiard room, populated entirely by men. He took off his jacket and waited for the next game to start. But sitting in the large leather recliner in the corner, a warm fire crackling, the sounds of the party muffled by the thick wooden doors, wasn't a good idea. He was nodding off when the doors opened.

"Told you," Dean said, slapping Jared on the shoulder.

"Hiding out?" Jared asked.

Spencer shrugged. "Figured I'd wait to play."

When the table cleared, they jumped up, racked up the balls and rolled up their sleeves. On the second round, Dean was chalking his pool cue when he said, "Let's make this interesting."

Jared chuckled. "I was waiting."

Spencer frowned. "Now what?"

"I win, I get to kiss Tatum under the mistletoe. You win, you do," Dean suggested.

Spencer's frown grew. "No."

"I could just do it," Dean said. "This way I'm giving you a chance to stop me."

Spencer sighed. Knowing Tatum, she'd let him kiss her on the cheek. Dean was already getting what he wanted: Spencer's reaction. "Fine." He forced the word out.

Spencer lost.

As Dean grinned at him, Spencer shrugged him off. His cousin didn't need to know that he wanted to punch him in the face.

"Come on, boys, they're about to cut the cake," his mother said, poking her head in the door. "Honestly, it's your brother's engagement party not a pool hall." She ducked back out, leaving the door wide.

But Spencer lingered, putting the table back to rights before reluctantly heading into the library. It took seconds to find her. Her hair fell over one shoulder, one hand holding a glass of white wine, the other resting on her lap. She was talking to an older gentleman, her hand lifting to emphasize the point she was making. The man said something in return and they both smiled.

She was beautiful.

"Hey," Lucy said, nudging him. "You're staring."

"Yep," he said. Because she was beautiful.

"Stop," she said, giggling.

"Do I have to?" he asked, glancing at her with a smile.

"How's work?" she asked.

"I won't be visiting your couch anytime soon." He sighed. "But there's still no word on Clint Taggart. Gotta feel for his wife and kids."

"How long has he been gone?" Lucy asked.

"Five days. Maybe six. His wife thought he'd gone on assignment. She didn't know he'd lost his job." He finished his beer. Not knowing had to suck. "Anything new with you?"

"Nope. Spending most of my free time with Tatum." She paused. "Like you. Only without the sex and nakedness."

He almost choked on his beer.

"No judging here. Two consenting adults. All good." Lucy took a sip of her wine.

"Um. Thanks?" he said. "When did all the women in this family decide they could say whatever they wanted whenever they wanted?"

Lucy looked up at him. "You've been talking to Cady, haven't you?"

He shook his head. "Everyone has an opinion."

"Because we all want you happy," Lucy said.

His attention returned to Tatum. She was looking at him, her green eyes wide. She smiled at him and his heart thudded in his chest.

"Oh my God!" Cady's voice drew his attention. "This is too much, you guys," Cady continued, jumping up to hug Bianca and Zach.

Patton was reading the card, surprise clear on his face. "Two weeks in Italy?"

Spencer chuckled. "I got them pots."

Lucy laughed. "I got them towels. But they're very nice towels."

"Sheets," Tatum added as she walked over, laughing. "Embroidered, Egyptian cotton."

"Nice," he said, beyond pleased that she'd joined them.

"But Italy, wow." She shook her head.

"I know," Lucy agreed. "Talk about a honeymoon."

"Excuse me," Tatum said, slipping from the room.

He watched her go.

"Go on," Lucy said, pushing him toward the door with a smile.

TATUM SMILED AT the bartender as he filled her glass. "Thank you." She sat at the bar, scanning the empty dining room. Everyone was in the library. The quiet was a nice change.

"Not a fan of crowds?"

She heard Spencer's voice and smiled into her glass. She'd known he'd follow her. Wasn't that why she'd let him know she was leaving? "It was getting a little stuffy in there." She glanced at him, sitting on the bar stool next to her.

"Spencer." He held his hand out.

She hesitated, her brows arching. "Tatum?" So he wanted to play games? *Fine. Bring it.* Anticipation settled hot and sweet in the pit of her stomach.

"You sound like you're not sure." The gravel of his voice drove her crazy.

"Sorry, I...I thought we'd met before?" She waited but he just smiled at her. "Guess I had you confused with someone else." He was too good-looking, too intense. He looked at her like she was naked. She felt naked.

He shook his head. "I'd remember you."

She smiled slightly, buzzing with pure lust.

"Who?" he asked, his gaze fastened on her mouth.

"Who what?" she asked.

"Who did you think I was?"

She smiled. "This guy I'm sleeping with."

"Lucky guy," he said, still staring at her mouth.

Lucky her. Spencer was an incredible lover. "I was hoping he'd come tonight," she said, breathless.

"Why?" he asked. His gaze crashed into her.

"I've been thinking about him," she managed. She could do this. "He...he's really good with his hands."

He slammed his beer bottle down on the counter, making the bartender look up from his ledger at the end of the counter. She turned toward Spencer, away from the bartender, nervous enough without an audience.

"Just his hands?" he asked.

She shook her head. "And his mouth."

Spencer slid off his stool, standing so close heat rolled off of him. His hand rested on her knee, sliding beneath the wool of her skirt. His fingers slid higher, finding the edge of her stockings. He closed his eyes, his jaw locking hard. His fingers slid around, finding the silky straps of her garter belt. "Wear this for him?" he asked, so rough she shivered.

She nodded, knowing their behavior was reckless but beyond caring. She'd never ached like this before, never worried she'd lose control so easily. "Think he might like it?" she asked, slipping forward on the stool, forcing his hand higher.

His breath tickled her ear. "I need you. Now," he growled, pressing her hand along the zipper of his slacks. Her fingers stroked his rigid length, making him swallow.

His fingers dipped higher and then he froze.

She wasn't wearing any panties.

"Dammit all to hell, Tatum," he muttered.

She moaned softly, turning her face into his neck as her fingers explored his impressive girth. She stroked him, again and again, wishing he was buried inside her—

"Don't," he growled, grabbing her hand and tugging her off the bar stool.

"Here." She pressed a room key into his hand.

The shock on his face was pure victory. For a split second she thought he'd kiss her now. She wanted him to. Even knowing someone could walk in any second. She walked from the bar, knowing he'd follow, knowing he was just as eager to get to the room as she was.

When they reached the door, he fumbled with the lock. Once the door swung open, his hands were on her. She heard the door slam as he pressed her against the heavy wood. He stared down, yanking her skirt up around her waist to reveal her satin garters and no panties. His broken curse, almost a plea, made her weak.

"Look at me," he growled, his knee nudging her legs apart.

She did, her breath escaping in short gasps.

He kissed her, his tongue invading her mouth as two long fingers sunk deep inside of her. She rocked back on her heels, tilting to take more. His thumb found her, stroking her, driving her mad. Her head fell back against the door as her body surrendered. Her hands clutched his arm, riding his hand, his fingers, lost to the stroke of his thumb. She was trembling, convulsing around his fingers. She shook her head, drowning in him.

He kissed her, latching on to her lower lip.

His thumb grazed her sweetly tortured flesh and she climaxed. She buried her face against his chest, muffling her scream as best she could.

When her trembling eased, his fingers left her.

She opened her eyes to watch him back up, slipping his tie free. He was gasping, his chest heaving as he stared at her exposed body. She steadied herself and moved forward, unzipping her skirt and letting it fall on the floor. She tugged her sweater off, striding toward him.

She tore his shirt open, mindless of the buttons that popped and bounced across the room. When his chest was bare, her lips descended. His taste, his scent, stoked her already raging hunger. Without thought, she unbuttoned his pants, sighing as her hands pushed the fabric down. She cupped his ass, raking her nails along his skin.

He shivered, gripping her arms and tugging her close.

She kissed him, opening her mouth for him. His tongue was magic, fierce and demanding, greedy—the way she wanted him. His fingers fumbled with the closure of her bra before he cupped her exposed breast in his large hands. She leaned into him, embracing the frenzy of want between them.

She pushed him toward the bench at the end of the bed, smiling as he sat. "Lie back," she said, her voice husky. He did, his gaze blazing into hers. He lay there, gripping the legs of the bench while she straddled him—still wearing her boots and garter belt.

He closed his eyes as she arched forward, feeling every inch of him push deep inside. She moaned, rocking forward. Her knees hung off the side of the bench, her heels buried in the carpet. She had all the leverage, all the power. And she used it to her advantage.

His reaction fueled her overwhelming craving to control. He quivered beneath her, clenched with each thrust, hissing and cussing and groaning. The throb of him, the heated friction, the brush of skin on skin. His body was a work of art, all rough angles and smooth contours.

He sat up, lightly biting her shoulder, licking her neck. His lips latched on to her nipple, his tongue flicking the sensitized flesh and making her cry out.

She ground against him, wanting control. It wasn't fair that he could invade her body and steal her senses. She wanted to make him fall apart. She rested her hands on his knees, setting a frenetic pace. The muscle of his thighs tightened, his fingers biting into her sides, as he moved beneath her. His arms wound around her, supporting her as he drove into her.

His strangled moan, the pulse of him convulsing inside her, split her apart.

He held her in place as she rode out her climax.

How he managed to stand, she didn't know. One minute they were upright, the next, she was lying on his chest, the feel of cool sheets covering them.

She felt the rapid beat of his heart echoing her own. She knew this heart and loved the sound of it. Whatever she and Brent had had, it had never compared to what she'd felt for Spencer. She'd loved him down to the cellular level. His hands came up, smoothing her hair down her back in long strokes. She closed her eyes, reveling in the feel of him. The scent of him.

"You okay?" he asked breathlessly.

She nodded. She was good. So good she didn't want to move.

She felt him press a kiss to the top of her head. She looked up at him then, resting her chin in the middle of his chest. She covered his chest with her hand, staying connected to him. This connection had been her strength and her downfall. Now…she didn't know what it meant. She'd wanted this to be about sex, about freedom, but she knew it was more.

His fingers slid through her hair as his eyes bored into hers. He swallowed.

"I thought…" She sucked in a deep breath, the words coming without thought. "When I moved to California, there were days I didn't know how to…to live. Or function."

His heart seemed to stop. Then start up again, faster than ever.

"I thought there was something wrong with me—"

He shook his head. "No."

She placed a finger over his lips. "And there was. I poured all of my love, everything I had, into you. So when we were done, I had to accept I was wrong…to learn what love was. To remember that I couldn't let myself feel like that ever again."

He closed his eyes.

"That's why ending my marriage didn't destroy me. So thank you for that."

He looked at her then, his face so rigid and remote. He tried to sit up, but she shook her head, her hand firmly pressed to his heart. He covered her hand with his.

"That's why you and I can't have more than this. I know I wouldn't survive this time." But explaining why she could never love him didn't change the fact that she already did.

10

SPENCER HELD HER against him. He'd scarred her. Left her broken. "I'm sorry, Tatum. I'm so damn sorry."

She stared up at him.

"I did what I thought I had to do," he said.

She frowned then, confusion marring her features. "What are you talking about?"

"I hurt you when I should have fought for you," he confessed.

She tried to move, but he held her in place.

He knew he was entering dangerous territory but he wanted her to know the truth. "I knew you wouldn't leave unless I made you." His words turned gruff and hard.

She froze. "What?"

"Your mother—"

She held up her hand. "Don't. She has nothing to do with this."

"She has everything to do with this. I know it bothers you to talk about her. But it bothered me to know she was hurting you. I saw the bruises, Tatum," he argued. "And I couldn't live with it."

"Let me go, Spencer," she said softly.

He did.

She slipped from the bed, dragging the quilt with her. "I don't understand." She sat on the bench, her boots peeking out between the folds of the blanket. He waited. He should have kept his mouth shut, apologized without spilling his guts.

How many times had he woken up, dripping sweat and hating himself? If he could go back in time, he would handle it differently. He was a stupid kid who was trying to save the girl he loved. Breaking up with her hadn't been the worst part of it. Having her come back, day after day, asking him to give them another chance. *Whatever I've done, I can fix it.* Her words had shredded him. She wouldn't give up on him, on them.

"But you said... You said..." She looked so lost.

"I lied. I lied to get you out of here and away from your mother."

"She was depressed, sick— She couldn't control her moods. She didn't know what she was doing, Spencer—"

"It didn't matter." He shook his head, sliding from the bed to stand before her. "She hurt *you*, mentally and physically. Don't you remember how it was with us, Tatum? How much I loved you? I would have done anything, *anything*, to protect you."

She stared at him, swallowing. "You used *her* words to drive me away? You told me there was something wrong with me." She choked on the words.

There's something wrong with you, Tatum. Fix it, or no one will ever love you, not really. He'd heard Tatum's mom say them and felt the pain of those words. It wasn't the woman's fault that she was bipolar. But Tatum was the one that suffered when Jane Buchanan forgot to take her meds. Tatum was the one who cleaned up after her mother when she had a temper fit. Tatum was the one who took the abuse.

"I was all she had," Tatum said. "If I'd stayed—"

"No, you staying wouldn't have kept her alive." Spencer shook his head. "It would have destroyed you."

"You did a pretty good job," she whispered. "Because of you... Spencer, I believed you. *You* had never lied to me. You had promised...promised me..." She shook her head. "I could deal with my mom. I understood why my dad couldn't deal. But you? You were my safe haven. And hearing you say that to me...that was the first time I ever felt alone."

Her words wrapped around his heart, a vise of barbed wire.

She stood, finding her clothes and increasing his panic.

He stopped her, blocking her path. "I have no excuse. Only regrets. Every damn day for eight years I've thought about you, knowing I'd lost the best thing to ever happen to me. What I did was wrong but I can't undo it—no matter how much I wish I could." He paused, watching the play of emotions on her face. "Your dad wanted you in California, remember? You said no. Because of me. I was responsible. I was the reason you were being hurt over and over. Losing you was like cutting out my heart. But... I had to. I had to—"

She shook her head. "No, you didn't. Not like that. You were deliberately cruel. You knew my weakness and you used that against me." She sucked in a deep breath.

"If I'd asked you to go, would you?" he asked.

She opened her mouth, her brow creasing. "How can I know that? What difference does it make? You didn't just take away my choices. You made me doubt myself—my worth."

"I was a seventeen-year-old idiot who loved you—" He broke off.

"And I was the idiot who valued your opinion more than anyone else's."

It was hard to breathe. "I'm asking for your forgiveness. Maybe, in time, some understanding." If he told her he loved her, would it make a difference? "You deserve all the love, all the happiness a man can give you. You are amazing. Thoughtful, kind, beautiful. I'm sorry that my actions caused you to doubt that."

She stared at him. "I need you to leave. Now." She closed herself in the bathroom.

He dressed quickly, sighing at the sight of his shirt. Once he was dressed, he stared at the bathroom door. She was mad, and she had every right to be mad. She needed time and space. He'd give it to her.

He slipped from the room and headed to the coatroom, sliding into his blazer and buttoning it up before getting a beer and heading back to the party. If he was smart he'd leave. But he couldn't, not yet.

He ignored the questioning looks of Lucy and Patton, pretending his cousins' debate on V-6 versus V-8 engines held his attention. Thirty minutes and another beer later, Tatum arrived. Not only did she avoid making eye contact, she seemed determined to stay at least ten feet away from him at all times.

"What the hell did you do?" Patton asked.

"Don't ask." He glanced her way, willing her to look at him.

But she didn't look his way.

She spent the next few minutes helping his mother

pack up the presents for Cady and Patton. And another few minutes talking to the same older gentleman she'd been talking to before. He was saying his goodbyes when he saw Dean making his way to her.

She smiled at him, listening as his cousin undoubtedly tried to charm her. He looked at the floor at his feet, the wave of anger surprising him.

Patton said, "Tried to talk to her?"

He nodded.

"Did you talk to Lucy first?" Patton asked.

He glared at his brother. "What for?"

"She's a shrink. And a woman. Might have prevented the arctic treatment."

Spencer sighed, wishing he could take back the last hour. "Too late now."

"I can see that." Patton's pale eyes were fixed at the doorway.

Spencer glanced over in time to see Dean point up at the mistletoe he'd led her under. He should look away. He should ignore it and let it go. He'd won the bet, so of course he was going to try to rub Spencer's face in it. She'd turn and give him her cheek… Except she didn't. She was kissing him. Her arms were loose around his neck, her lips lingering on Dean's…

"Breathe," Patton reminded him.

"I'm breathing," he snapped.

But he couldn't look away. Tatum's smile. Dean's startled, but very pleased, expression.

"Go," Patton said. "Mom'll kick your ass if you started a fight."

He nodded, moving across the room as unobtrusively as possible. So why did it feel like everyone was staring at him?

He threw his truck into gear and drove into town, heading straight for Zeke's gym. It was late and the weather was bad, but there were plenty of guys willing to spar with him. After a quick warm-up he climbed into the ring and cut loose.

They had to take turns, giving him just enough time to catch his breath, stop whatever was bleeding and go again. When the gym closed at midnight, he drove to his mother's and the beat-up sleeper sofa in the near-arctic garage. Hell, at this point, it didn't matter where he slept as long as he could sleep. No matter what, he'd feel like total shit in the morning.

He hadn't been expecting to find his brothers waiting for him on the front porch.

He put the truck in Park and climbed the steps.

"Need a place to sleep?" Patton asked.

"Nah." He shook his head. "Garage."

"It's freaking cold," Zach said. "Let's go."

Spencer nodded, leading them into the garage and flipping on the lights. Folding chairs were located, a space heater was plugged in and Zach produced a large bottle of whiskey.

"Go to Zeke's?" Patton asked, pulling cups from their camping gear.

He nodded. "Is it bad?"

Zach and Patton exchanged looks.

"Make for some interesting wedding pictures," Zach said, laughing.

Spencer sighed. "Dammit."

Patton shrugged. "Fine by me." He poured out drinks.

There was a comfortable silence as they all knocked back their alcohol.

"Dean wanted to come," Zach offered, earning a hard glance from Patton.

"Not his fault," Spencer said, emptying the glass. "It's me."

Patton sipped his drink, flopping into one of the chairs and scooting closer to the heater. "Bad?"

He nodded.

"She hasn't really been here long enough for you to screw it up *that* bad." Zach sat in one of the other chairs.

He paced, the whiskey and the cold keeping him moving. "I screwed up. The sort of long-term, psychological shit that takes years to get over. And even if she gets over it, chances are she's never going to love me."

"And that's what we want?" Zach clarified.

"Yes, Zach." Patton sighed. "Do you listen to a thing I say?"

"No, not really." Zach smiled.

Spencer chuckled. "Remember our breakup?" he asked.

"The one where you were basically catatonic for a year?" Zach asked. "Yeah, good times."

Spencer flipped him off.

"That was a hell of a long time ago." Patton crossed his arms over his chest.

"I know we were kids, but I loved her. I mean, she was everything. Losing her was a nightmare. I believed we were forever. It felt like it would be. But if you love someone like that, you have to put them first, right?" He barely looked at them. "Her mom used to abuse her. Mostly mentally, but she got hit too. Tatum would make excuses, forgive her, but it ate at her—tore her down. And no matter how much I told her Dad could help, or the school could help, she felt responsible for her mom. Her mom used the guilt card a lot. Her dad kept asking her to come live with him, but she wouldn't go. Because of me."

Patton ran a hand over his face.

Zach set his empty glass on the floor. "So you dumped her."

Spencer nodded, sitting on the edge of the lumpy couch. "I made Dad call her father in California when she wouldn't leave. She wasn't safe here and I couldn't let it go on."

"I know you guys were pretty serious," Zach said, leaning forward. "So I'm assuming you pulled out the big guns for this breakup?"

"Cheating rumors." Patton glanced his way.

"Ouch," Zach said.

"Worse." He dropped his head in his hands. "Her mom…her mom used to say there was something wrong with her. That she needed to fix it or no one would ever love her. I said it to drive her away."

"Aw, shit, Spence," Zach groaned. "That's just mean. And teenage girls… I mean. You're king of the assholes."

"Why say anything now?" Patton asked.

"She said I was right." He shook his head. "She said that our relationship taught her never to love that much again. I had to tell her what I'd done. I had to."

Zach groaned.

Patton sighed.

He didn't bother lifting his head.

"So you begged for forgiveness?" Patton asked.

"On your knees?" Zach added.

"You saw how well that went," Spencer murmured. "I probably wouldn't forgive me, either."

"We need more whiskey," Zach said, reaching for the bottle. "It's gonna be a long night."

TATUM HAD NEVER had a hangover before. Everything ached. Her head, her eyes, her eyelids.

"Drink this," Celeste said, putting a glass of something green on the table in front of her.

"What is it?" she asked, her tongue thick and heavy.

"You drank all of these?" Lucy asked, scraping the army of miniature alcohol bottles into the trash. "Vodka. And tequila. Did you throw up?"

"Not yet." Tatum pressed a hand to her stomach. "Not to be rude, but why are you all here?"

"We'd talked about looking at the tearoom books, remember?" Celeste patted her hand.

"And you'd volunteered to make dessert tonight and, after last night, we thought we could help." Lucy sighed.

Accounting? She almost groaned. Baking? Dessert. For dinner. Tonight. At the Ryans' house. She groaned. Before they went caroling. Because she'd promised Mrs. Ryan at the auxiliary auction. "Oh, God."

"It's okay," Lucy said. "We've got plenty of time. It's only eleven."

Tatum covered her face with her hands. "So you're checking up on me?" she asked.

"Yes," Celeste admitted.

"I'm fine." She slid the glass across the table, sipping from the top. "That's awful."

"It is," Celeste agreed. "But it will settle your stomach."

She sipped again. "This is awkward."

"Why?" Lucy asked. "We've all been there. Men can be…morons."

"The question is, what can we do?" Celeste asked. "I'm a doer."

Tatum shook her head. "I was going to bake a black forest cake…" She covered her mouth.

"You have everything?" Celeste asked, hopping up and opening the refrigerator.

She nodded, pointing.

"Recipe?" Lucy asked.

She shook her head and tapped her forehead. "Secret."

They froze.

"Seriously?" Lucy asked.

Tatum shook her head, laughing weakly. "Red cookbook." She pointed.

"You're a hoot," Lucy said, squeezing her shoulder gently.

Celeste turned off the overhead lights. "Better?"

Tatum nodded. "Can you see?" she asked, peering through bloodshot eyes.

"Yep," Celeste said, already pulling out bowls.

"This sounds yummy," Lucy said as she read the recipe.

She sat, sipping her green concoction, strangely soothed by Lucy and Celeste's presence. At some point, she took a pain reliever. She felt almost civilized after the cake was in the oven and they made her take a shower.

But she emerged to find them standing, staring curiously at all the pictures, newspaper clippings, trinkets and one almost shredded pom-pom scattered around her room. In fact, her room looked like a bomb had exploded. She didn't remember much. She'd come home so angry, so confused. Apparently she'd taken it out on her room.

Stubbing her foot on the shoe box full of travel liquor at the bottom of the hall closet had seemed like an answer to her anger. Worse than anger was pain.

"You were a cute cheerleader," Celeste said, holding up a newspaper clipping.

Tatum sat on her bed. "I don't remember doing this."

"You drank a lot," Lucy offered, stooping to pick up the bits of paper and photos scattered all over the room.

"I had been planning on cleaning out the room," she muttered.

"I'll get a box," Lucy said. "No point in putting this stuff back up." She returned with the empty shoe box.

"I didn't drink all of it?" she gasped.

"No. You'd be dead." Celeste's smile was concerned. "I put it in the kitchen cabinet."

"We can throw it away?" Lucy offered.

"Don't worry," Tatum assured her. "I've so learned my lesson."

"Is this Spencer?" Celeste asked, offering the photo to Tatum.

She took it. "Yes." She stared at the image, her eyes burning with hot tears. She didn't need to look at it to know what it was. It was a picture she'd had pegged up above her bed. It was old and they were young. She was sitting on a chair and he was sitting on the floor between her legs. Her hand was at an awkward angle, because he was holding it. But what made it so special was the naturalness of Spencer pressing a kiss, almost absentmindedly, to her hand. Second nature. Like breathing.

He'd felt the same way, she'd known it—never doubted it. Until he'd…he'd crushed her heart. But now she knew the truth. He hadn't been some thoughtless hormonal teenage boy. No, he had to have the noblest of motivations. He was trying to save her. To protect her. Because he'd loved her.

Losing you was like cutting out my heart…

And just like that she was sobbing.

"Oh, Tatum." Lucy sounded heartbroken.

"Don't make yourself sick." Celeste ran from the room, reappearing with a cool, wet cloth. "Here."

Tatum pressed the cloth to her face, mortified.

"You can talk about it," Lucy prompted. "We won't say anything."

"I don't know if I—I can talk about it," she forced out.

"Then we don't have to," Lucy said.

Tatum nodded, her brain swimming. It took her a while to ask, "Could you forgive a person for lying to you about something?"

"Depends on what it was," Celeste said. "Some things are unforgivable."

Tatum nodded.

"I'd disagree," Lucy said. "If we're talking about a person you love, almost anything is forgivable."

Tatum glanced at the picture. "What if the person you loved most, the person who knew all of your secrets, used your weakness to drive you away?"

"Can you, maybe, give us a little more to go on?" Celeste asked.

Tatum did. From him telling her he didn't love her anymore to that horrible scene in the cafeteria when he said those words—the words that echoed in her ears for months after she'd moved to California. "There's something wrong with you, Tatum…" He'd kept going, saying her mother's words while his arm draped along some other girl's shoulders. "You need to let go. Move on. I don't love you anymore." She'd stood there, staring at him, wanting to scream.

"Why?" Lucy asked, her cheeks red. "Why was he so determined to make you leave?"

That was the part she had a hard time confessing. She knew her mother hadn't treated her well, that Spencer was right. But she'd spent so many years fooling herself. Her mother was ill, alone. She had to stay—to love her. No one else would. It was only after Spencer had broken her heart, after her father had shown up determined to take her with him and her mother into a treatment facility, that she relented. Leaving had been a relief.

"My mom…" She drew in a deep breath. "Spencer was trying to get me away from my mom."

They waited.

"Because she was mean to me."

"Mean to you?" Celeste repeated, her eyes going round.

"Oh, Tatum." Lucy hugged her. "People talked but I never thought… Why didn't you say anything?"

She shook her head.

"So he was a complete ass," Celeste murmured, "because he loved you."

"And when he found out he'd left scars, he wanted to make it better." Lucy was on the verge of tears. "Because he still loves you. Why else would he feel the need to tell you the truth now?"

Tatum froze, going numb. No. He didn't love her. He couldn't love her. He wanted her. "Maybe he just needed to clear his conscience?" But she wasn't sure she believed that. If Spencer wasn't the heartless bastard she'd thought, who was he? Too many years had gone by for him to be her Spencer. No, *not* her Spencer.

Her head throbbed. It didn't matter. She had a hangover—that was why she was emotional. Spencer, the past, none of it mattered. It couldn't. With him, she was… vulnerable. Vulnerable and needy. She didn't want to be either.

"What are you going to do?" Celeste asked.

She shrugged.

"What do you want?" Lucy asked. "That's where you need to start. If he does love you, it makes more sense for you to know what you want first."

She nodded, sniffing the air. "Chocolate."

"Always a good place to start," Lucy agreed, laughing.

"The cake." Celeste hopped up, running into the kitchen.

She looked at Lucy.

"Where was I?" Lucy asked. "Why wasn't I there?" She shook her head. "I should have been there to back you up, to scream at him when you wouldn't."

"Different lunch periods." She shrugged. "I called my dad as soon as I got home."

"That was the weekend you left." Lucy looked at her. "That horrible weekend. Spencer fell apart."

"I'm not going to feel sorry for him right now, okay? Not yet." Tatum flopped back on her bed. "Why do we make things more complicated than they need to be?"

Lucy flopped back with her. "Human nature, I think." She looked at her. "Are you going to come tonight? To dinner and caroling?"

Tatum closed her eyes. "I don't think so. I need time to pull it together. Right now, the only thing I know is my heart hurts."

11

SHE SKIPPED DINNER and caroling, claiming a headache. But when they stopped by, she wrapped herself in a blanket and stood on the porch to listen. She hadn't seen Spencer, but she'd felt his absence.

The next day Lucy came over and helped her start weeding through things. It wasn't as bad as she thought it would be. Brent had hired a professional organizer after her mother's death. They'd done an exceptional job of clearing out every piece of clothing, shoes, toiletries... Almost all signs of her mother. There were three large boxes she and Lucy tackled together. But there wasn't much. Mostly pictures and keepsakes gathered from before her father had left them. Nothing from Tatum's high school years, none of the letters Tatum had written when she and Brent had settled in his hometown.

When she'd pulled all the things she wanted, they'd hauled the boxes onto the front porch.

"I can call Dean?" Lucy offered. "He has a truck."

Tatum shook her head. "No, please don't. I feel terrible for what I did. I can't keep leading him on."

"You kissed him under the mistletoe." Lucy nudged her. "I didn't see tongue, or groping."

Tatum laughed. "Because there wasn't any."

"Then you're fine."

They sat on her front porch swing, enjoying the crisp air. Even though her yard was coated in a layer of white snow, the sun was shining down.

"It's a beautiful day," she said.

"It is," Lucy agreed. "But I'm starving. I think I'll order a pizza."

A faint thud from across the street drew her attention. Spencer was carrying a duffel bag, headed toward his truck. She watched him open the large toolbox in his truck bed, rifling through it before closing it again. He grabbed the bag, opened the truck door and tossed it inside.

He slammed the door and looked across the street.

She froze, panic sinking in. She wasn't ready to deal with him, not yet.

He lifted his hand in a wave.

Lucy waved back.

After a moment's hesitation, he headed across the street. And every step he took stirred up some new, conflicting emotion. It was easier when she just wanted him. Now…she shook her head. That *was* all. She wanted him. Nothing else. *Want* might be an understatement. Her body craved him like her lungs craved air.

He was red-nosed when he climbed the steps to her porch. But all she could see was the huge bruise along his right cheek, the taped cut on his eyelid and the gash across the bridge of his nose. She was up, reaching for his face before she realized what she was doing. "What happened?"

He stared down at her, closing his eyes as her fingers touched the bruise. "It's nothing," he said gruffly.

She blinked, pulling her hand back. He had a dangerous job. This probably wasn't all that unusual. "Tell me this has nothing to do with Dean." Had she caused a rift between him and his cousin?

He snorted. "Dean didn't do this. He wouldn't have gotten in this many punches."

Relief washed over her. Not that she preferred him getting beaten up on the job.

He saw the boxes on the porch and frowned, his whole demeanor changing. His jaw locked, his hand—resting on the porch railing—tightened around the wood. "Going somewhere?" His voice broke—she heard it.

And when his blue eyes locked with hers it was impossible to breathe.

He had no right to look…like that. Like he cared. Like she'd hurt him. He had no right to make her hurt for him. Words failed her, so she stared at him, confused and frustrated. And angry.

She was vaguely aware of Lucy saying, "I think I need to go pick up the pizza," before she left.

Spencer's gaze bounced from her to the boxes and back again. He seemed braced, waiting for something.

She opened her mouth, then closed it. She didn't know what to say. Or how to read him. After last night, everything seemed upside-down. Only one thing was certain— she wasn't up for any more life-altering revelations.

So why did she want to reach out for him? Maybe it was the wariness on his face or the hint of sadness in his eyes… Whatever it was, she wanted to comfort him. *Dammit.* She hugged herself.

His voice was rough. "Tatum—"

"On your way to work?" she asked, cutting him off before more things were said.

He sighed, his eyes narrowing. "Not until tonight." What was he looking for?

"Oh, well…" She stepped back, putting space between them. "Good time to get your Christmas shopping done… or something." Since she couldn't seem to be near him without touching him, she needed to remove herself. Her fingers were already longing to trace his stubble-covered jaw, to press a kiss to the corner of his mouth, to hold him close until his posture eased. All of which were very bad ideas. "See you later," she said, stepping around him and going inside.

But once she was inside, she froze. She didn't want to think or get emotional, but she didn't want him to leave. *Don't go.* She swallowed down the knot of fear and sucked in a deep breath. "Shit… Spencer—" she called out.

He was through the door in an instant, closing the distance between them as he pressed her against the entry-way wall. She wrapped her arms around his neck, pressing her mouth to his. She wanted his kiss, his tongue, his touch—she craved him beyond reason.

His arms were steel around her, lifting her. She wrapped her legs around his waist and held on.

"I couldn't sleep last night, couldn't think." He cupped her face between his hands, pinning her with the raw hunger of his gaze. "I need you so bad it hurts."

She tugged his hair, ignoring all the possible ways she could interpret his words. It was easier to pull his head back to hers. He devoured her mouth, stealing her breath, making her light-headed. He carried them to her room, kissing her as though his life depended on it. She wanted him like this, fierce and hungry for her. Once she was pinned between him and her bedroom door, she reached down between them, unbuttoning his pants. His gaze bored into hers as her fingers freed him from his boxers. Her fingers wrapped around him, slowly. He was hot to the touch, smooth.

He let go of her long enough to tug her pants off. And then he was there, lifting her, his hands bracing her hips, parting her so he could fill her in one thrust. They groaned together, the sweet friction pulling her under. She smiled, her head falling back against the wall, savoring each stroke against her inflamed flesh.

"Don't stop." She pressed her ankles into his buttocks.

"I won't," he said, nipping her earlobe.

He didn't. His face was hard, driven, as he set a deep and frantic rhythm. His barely restrained hunger made her tremble. Her nails dug into his hips, mindless in her need. When he caught her lower lip with his teeth, she came apart. Hard. Fast. Out of control. It was oh so good. "Spencer," she gasped, shuddering at the aftershocks that rippled through her.

She wrapped her arms around his neck, pressing her forehead to his. She relished the rough groan that tore from his throat as he stiffened.

Seconds later she was lying on her bed, gasping, with Spencer at her side. Her mind was spinning, returning to her preorgasmic state of equal parts panic, frustration… and love. She closed her eyes, draping her arm across her forehead.

She understood why he'd done what he did. Their connection wasn't just physical. He had known her better than anyone else, had known she was hurting, and did what he had to, to stop it. She would have done the same.

She loved him. So much it scared her.

If she was smart, she'd keep her mouth shut. She didn't want to be hurt anymore. Heartfelt confessions and desire-fueled promises were all fine and good now, when they were still wrapped in discovery and lust. But there was no way this was real. That this could last. It was too…big.

No matter what Lucy believed, he'd never said he loved her, not in so many words. And while she was willing to accept what he'd done was because he'd once loved her—that didn't mean he still did. No, better to keep things as they were. It would hurt less this way.

She glanced at him and smiled.

He was sound asleep, snoring ever so softly. And he was gorgeous. This man was the boy she'd loved completely. He'd been lean and awkward then, but he'd loved her with a confidence that told her it was right. And she'd been too young to know better. With him, she'd never doubted herself or felt alone.

Until she did.

She studied his profile, the line of his brow, the angle of his jaw, thick brows and full lips. She ran a finger along his forehead, smoothing his hair back. He sighed, turning into her in his sleep.

Dammit.

If Lucy wasn't due back soon, she'd have no problem staying as she was. But Lucy *was* coming back, so pants were required. She felt Spencer's hand twitch and looked down. His hand held hers.

HE WOKE TO Christmas carols, laughter and singing.

It took a minute to orient himself. He was in Tatum's bed, alone, covered in blankets.

A shout of laughter made him grin. Tatum and Lucy, from the sounds of it.

He kicked back the blankets, ran a hand through his hair and glanced at the clock. It was almost 6:00 p.m. He had an hour before he needed to be at the station. He turned on the bedside lamp and stretched. It had been a long time since he'd slept a solid five hours without waking. It made sense that he'd done it in Tatum's bed. It was the one place he could truly relax.

He glanced around the room, taking in the changes. The pom-pom and trophies were gone. The walls were bare. Even the curtains had been pulled down. He remembered the boxes on the front porch, the tightness in his chest making it hard to breathe. Was she really packing up? She hadn't answered him. And it gnawed at his gut. He rubbed his hands over his face and rolled his neck. What would he do if she left?

More important, how did he convince her to stay?

He caught sight of the romance novel on her bedside table and picked it up. He shook his head at the cover and flipped it over to read the back. Something slipped from the pages and fell to the floor. He stooped to pick it up. A picture.

He stared at the picture, his heart thumping. A picture of them. They were on a field trip somewhere. One of the journalist students had snapped the picture and given a copy to each of them.

In a room intentionally stripped of all sentimentality, why was this picture out? This was something she'd held on to. Hope crashed into him. And happiness. He tucked the picture beneath the book and stood, heading into the kitchen.

Lucy and Tatum were in pajamas, sliding around the kitchen floor in fuzzy socks. Tatum's kitten-covered pink thermal pajamas and pigtails had him shaking his head.

She looked gorgeous, swinging a large wooden spoon around as she belted out Mariah Carey Christmas carols at the top of her lungs.

Lucy joined in, adding sprinkles to some of the stacks and stacks of cookies that covered the kitchen countertops. Among the tubes of icing and bottles of sprinkles, a gigantic gingerbread house was being built.

He leaned against the door, smiling. When they finished their performance, he clapped.

They both jumped.

Lucy burst out laughing. "Good to see you're alive and well. I was beginning to worry Tatum might have killed you."

Tatum glanced at him, cocking an eyebrow but not saying a word. Instead, the tip of her tongue licked a dollop of pink frosting from her spoon.

"She tried," he said, as he cleared his throat. Apparently they weren't keeping things a secret from Lucy.

Tatum frowned at him, dropping the spoon in the sink. "We made cookies."

"I see that." His brows rose. "I can eat a lot but—"

"They're for you to take to work," Tatum said. "It's Christmas."

As if that explained everything. She'd made cookies for him to take to work because it was Christmas. His smile grew.

"Her idea," Lucy said. "I just wanted to eat some cookie dough."

"They'll be appreciated." He winked at Lucy, content to watch Tatum fill a large storage container with festively decorated cookies.

"We're having a sleepover," Tatum said.

"Aren't you two a little old for sleepovers?" he asked, smiling.

"You're never too old for a sleepover," Lucy said, smiling sweetly at him.

"What's your schedule?" Lucy asked. "I know Juan's trying to get as many people to cover as possible—since the baby came early."

He nodded. "Not sure." But he hoped like hell he could avoid more overtime. His and Tatum's time was running out, and he wanted to make every second count. "It's been pretty slow."

"Spencer is sort of a hero right now. Did he tell you that?" Lucy asked Tatum. "Not that he brags on himself."

Tatum's eyes met his. "What did you do?"

He glared at Lucy. "Really?"

"Come on, Spencer, it's sweet." Lucy perched on the kitchen counter. "He was at the high school, doing some sort of don't-do-drugs thing when these boys got into a fight. He got in the middle of it, broke it up and saved one of the kids from choking to death."

Tatum looked horrified. "The other kid was trying to kill him?"

"No." Spencer sighed. "The dumb kid was sucking on a piece of candy. The fight broke out. He got punched. I guess he inhaled it when he got the wind knocked out of him."

Tatum smiled. "So you broke up a fight and did the Heimlich maneuver? I bet you made quite an impression."

"He made the front page of the paper. Aunt Imogene is framing it," Lucy said.

"What happened to the kids?" Tatum asked.

"I guess seeing his buddy turn blue made the other guy cool off real fast. They were all hugging and saying

'I'm sorry, man.'" Spencer laughed. "You couldn't pay me to be a teenage boy again. Too volatile."

Tatum giggled, staring pointedly at his injuries. "Hey, what's that on your face?"

He frowned.

"Y'all are fun." Lucy laughed.

"Pizza?" Tatum pulled a plate from the oven. "Sit, if you have time? It's veggie."

He shook his head. "I'll eat it in the truck. I should be heading out."

She wrapped the pizza in foil and set it on the container full of cookies. "Well…be careful."

He crossed the room, taking the container from her. "I will." He set the container on the counter, cupped her face in his hands and kissed her. He liked the startled look on her face, the perfect O her mouth made right before his lips met hers. She was so soft, so sweet. He broke away with a sigh. He pulled her close, sliding his hands up and down her back. "I promise," he whispered in her ear.

He grabbed his cookies and left, knowing a smart man would call in sick and crash their sleepover. He could decorate cookies with the best of them. Since his mother had no daughters, her boys all had basic cooking, cleaning and dancing skills. She considered all three of equal importance when it came to being a good spouse. As it was, he knew he was needed on the job—and hoped she'd let him make up for lost time later.

He drove to the station with the windshield wipers on high. After a sun-filled day, the sudden dip in the temperature and steady rain promised slick roadway conditions.

"Looks like tonight's going to be fun," he murmured, munching his pizza on the way to the station. Veggie or not, it was good.

He carried the cookies, nodding at his team as he headed toward his desk. After hanging his coat on the hook by his workstation, he shifted a stack of papers and put the container on the edge of his desk.

"I know you didn't make them," Patton said, pulling a cookie out.

"Nope." Spencer smiled. "Tatum did."

Patton grinned.

"Aren't you supposed to be off?" Spencer asked.

Patton shrugged, biting into the cookie. "Wrapping up a few loose ends."

"Patton, you could spend a month on loose ends." He pulled out the file he'd been working on. "Anything you need to catch me up on?"

"Where do I start?" Patton shook his head, sitting in the chair by Spencer's desk.

Spencer listened as Patton listed off what had rolled in since he'd left. There was a missing child linked to a known drug transporter—top priority. A neighborhood had over a dozen cars vandalized the night before, leaving a path of empty aerosol cans they were fingerprinting.

"Kids huffing?" Spencer asked. "Guess I'll check hospitals later, see if anyone turns up."

Patton nodded. "A twenty-four-year-old woman was found in the parking lot next to The Grind. Her blood work tested positive for Rohypnol, so they're doing a rape kit."

Spencer ran a hand over his face.

"And, last but not least, we have a van-load of teens in custody. They were coming back from a Dallas concert, smoke pouring out of their windows. Nothing like a moving hotbox to grab Highway Patrol's interest."

Spencer laughed. "People never fail to amaze me. They're damn lucky no one got killed."

"I don't remember what we were doing at that age, but I'd like to think we weren't that careless with other people's lives."

Spencer nodded. "We weren't. I can remember Zach trying to ski off the roof the year of the big blizzard. And I believe you—"

"Stopped you from breaking your neck more than once."

Spencer nodded, smiling. "Great. So I can expect a bunch of pissed-off parents who *know* it's not their kids' pot anytime?" Spencer asked, scanning over his notes. "The roofie thing, that's the third one this month."

Patton nodded, frowning.

"Any MO?" Spencer asked. "Same victim profile?"

Patton shook his head. "Doesn't appear so. Here." He handed him the file. "Feel free."

"What about the kid?" Spencer asked, looking at the whiteboard the clerk kept up as new information rolled in.

"It's a 1984 blue Dodge minivan with a gray bumper. We've had a few calls. Seems to be heading in our general direction." Patton sighed, staring at the abducted four-year-old girl's picture. "Sure would love to get her home safe."

Spencer nodded. "Custody thing?"

Patton nodded. "Dad lost rights because of his dealing. No one knows if he's using or not. And no violent record, just drugs. I'm hoping he's just a desperate dad doing a very stupid thing."

Spencer didn't say anything. Abduction cases were nasty, no matter what.

"Let me know if you hear something?" Patton asked.

Spencer nodded. "No news on Taggart?"

Patton shook his head, taking another cookie. "These are good."

"Are they?" He reached for one, popping it in his mouth. They were good. Not that he was surprised. Tatum had always liked to bake. Thinking of Tatum in her pink cat pajamas, pigtails bouncing, had him grinning from ear to ear.

"I take it she forgave you?" Patton asked, gathering his things up.

Spencer shook his head. "Not yet. But I'm working on it."

The intercom on his desk buzzed. "Got a call for backup. Immediate assistance requested to Cliffs Point and Jones Avenue."

"We're shorthanded, Spencer," Captain Ramirez yelled out.

"On it," Spencer answered, jumping up and tugging on his coat. "Go home to your fiancée, Patton. Take her a cookie." He winked as he sprinted out into the darkness.

12

"HELLO?" LUCY ANSWERED the phone while Tatum hunted for the remote control. "What's wrong, Aunt Imogene?"

A chill settled in Tatum's stomach. She flipped off the television and stood, suddenly too antsy to sit still.

"Which hospital? Glenn Oaks? Okay." Lucy's gaze met Tatum's. There was a long pause. "I'll come get you…Yes, she's here…What?…I'll tell her." She hung up her phone.

"Spencer?" she asked, already knowing the answer.

Lucy took her hands. "He's okay."

"What happened?" she asked, her voice trembling.

"Don't freak out, okay? He was stabbed—"

"Don't freak out?" she repeated. He'd been stabbed.

"It could be nothing, Tatum, really. He's in stable condition." Lucy stood, hurrying to the door.

"Nothing?" she asked. "You said he was *stabbed*."

"I'll let you know…" She paused. "He…he said for you not to come."

Tatum frowned. "Oh."

"I need to take Aunt Imogene. She can't drive on the

ice, too jumpy," she said, hugging her. "I'll let you know as soon as I know more."

Tatum nodded, feeling numb. "Okay."

Tatum stared out the front window, watching as Lucy and Mrs. Ryan piled into her car and drove off.

He was hurt. In a hospital. But he was in stable condition. Stable enough to tell her not to come. She hugged herself, hating how cold she felt.

If he didn't want her there she shouldn't go. He had a good reason.

She started cleaning up the mess she and Lucy had made in the kitchen. But once the kitchen was sparkling, there was still no word on Spencer. She texted Lucy, asking for an update, but she didn't get an answer.

Lucy would call her if it was bad. She'd call, period, wouldn't she? She'd know Tatum was worried.

But since Lucy wasn't texting her, she did a load of laundry and straightened the living room.

An hour and a half ticked by before she couldn't take it anymore. She put on her thick black coat, tugged on mittens and a hat, and climbed into the SUV. She plugged Glenn Oaks Hospital into her navigation system and drove, slipping along the icy roads. The closer she got, the more she shook. Which didn't help with driving on the icy roads.

When she rounded a corner, her tires locked and her SUV slid. But she relaxed, stayed calm and kept control. She recovered and came to a stop at the red light. As she rested her head on her steering wheel, terrified of what could have happened, she heard the screeching of brakes and looked up.

A truck slid across the intersection and plowed into her passenger side.

She barely had time to register what was happening as her SUV was forced across the road and slammed into a lamppost. Her head smacked the driver side window, cracking the glass and making her see stars. A horn was honking, but she didn't know if it was hers or the truck's. All she knew was it wouldn't stop.

She sat there, stunned, a warm stickiness running down the side of her face.

Her phone vibrated then, but she was too dazed to reach for it.

Someone knocked on the window. "You okay?"

"Yes," she said. "Just…hit my head."

"We called 9-1-1," the person said, trying to open her door. "Door's smashed in."

"I'm okay," she said again. She tried the door handle, but the door wouldn't move. "I'll climb over." But then she realized her passenger side was crumpled in on itself, the hood of the truck firmly embedded.

A young man tried to open her door. "You might want to stay put. In case you hurt your neck."

"I really think I'm okay," she said, trying to unbuckle her seat belt. She pressed the button but nothing happened. "My belt's stuck."

"Must be connected to the car's computer," the man said.

There were sirens.

"Just sit tight."

"I don't think I have a choice," she said, laughing softly. She reached up, feeling along her hairline. She winced, pulling back blood-covered fingers.

What an idiot. Spencer had told her not to come— probably for this very reason. Lucy had told her he was stable. But *no*, she just had to see for herself. And now this. She rested her head against the seat back.

Her phone vibrated again and this time she reached for it. Lucy.

Spencer's fine. Stitched at the scene and back at work. See, no worries. Want to finish the movie?

She laughed then, which made her head hurt.

"You okay?" the man asked.

"I'm fine," she assured him, though she doubted he could hear her over the blare of the sirens.

What was she doing? She'd dropped everything to get to Spencer—after he'd told her not to come. She was doing exactly what she didn't want to do. Getting too involved, too attached. And now she was bleeding and trapped in a car because of it. *I'm an idiot.* An idiot whose head was throbbing.

The paramedics managed to pry open the back door to reach her. One assessed her injuries, strapping a large foam brace around her neck before they helped her out of the passenger side. The firefighters had to cut through her seat belt and force her seat back to get her out. By then, her head was definitely hurting.

"How do you feel?" the paramedic asked.

Embarrassed. I sort of hate myself right now. Pathetic. "My head hurts."

He nodded. "You knocked your head pretty good," he said. "Might need a few stitches."

Stitches? She closed her eyes.

"I need you to stay awake for me," he said. "Just in case you have a concussion."

And a concussion? "Okay," she said.

"Can we call anyone?" he asked. "Next of kin?"

She swallowed. "Nope."

He blinked. "You sure?"

She tried not to glare at the man. "Believe me. I'm sure," she said. She had no one.

The ride in the ambulance was short—she'd almost been there when she'd had her accident. When they arrived in the emergency room, she answered the same questions over and over, had ten different people shine penlights in her eyes, made her touch her nose, walk a straight line and had her head x-rayed.

She had a concussion. And needed eight stitches behind her ear, which was swollen and sore.

"I'm going to have an elf ear for Christmas," she said to the ER nurse. "How festive."

"You'd look pretty no matter what," the woman said, smiling. "I'm Aileen. If you need anything, just holler. I'm your nurse. Okay?" She handed her the remote control. "You'll be staying with us for a while so might as well find something to entertain you." Aileen pulled the curtain back. "So I can keep an eye on you. No sleeping, okay?"

"Okay," Tatum said. She flipped channels. She couldn't feel her incision; it was numb. But the rest of her wasn't. Now that she wasn't trapped in a vehicle, in immediate peril, her brain decided to replay all the times she'd been hurt. Not stitches or concussion hurt, but brokenhearted and defeated hurt. Her father's desertion, her mother, Spencer, Brent... How many times did she have to fall flat to learn to stay on her guard?

Her divorce should have liberated her.

Sleeping with Spencer should have empowered her.

She was in control now. And somehow she'd forgotten that.

No matter what truths had come to light about Spencer and their past, she was still antirelationships. She didn't have the strongest evidence that loving someone was a good thing. The crisscross cuts and angry coloring of her right arm was example enough.

No more pretending things hadn't gotten way out of hand with Spencer. She only hoped she was strong enough to end it.

She aimlessly flipped the channels, unease and nausea setting her stomach on edge. News. Sports. Travel shows. *It's a Wonderful Life*. She stopped, knowing George Bailey's tale would cheer her up. With any luck, she'd be able to go home by the time the movie was over. If she was really lucky, she'd look into getting an earlier flight to California.

"SPENCER," HE ANSWERED his phone, eating another of Tatum's cookies. He'd been back at work for an hour, closing out two files, and four cookies. And every time he took a bite, his mind drifted to Tatum. Her smile. Her laugh. Her tongue licking icing off the spoon. It was a good damn thing he was at his desk tonight, because he'd be shit in the field.

"It's Jared." It was hard to hear his cousin over the background noise. "I just heard. Is she okay?"

"At work?" Spencer asked. "I can barely hear you."

"Is Tatum okay?" Jared repeated, enunciating.

Spencer sat forward, a knot forming in his throat. "As far as I know. Unless you know something I don't know?"

"Aw, shit," Jared sighed. "You don't know?"

"Know what?" Spencer asked. "What the hell do I not know?" He stood, staring around the station, his panic building.

"Tatum was taken to the emergency room—"

"Why?"

"Car accident."

Jared's words ripped the air from his lungs—more effective than a gut punch. The roads were ice slicks. Even with his four-wheel drive, he struggled. Tatum hadn't driven in these conditions in years—that was the reason he'd told her not to come see him. That, and there was no point. He was fine.

His heart twisted and his throat dried up. "When?"

"A couple of hours ago. Sorry, Spence, thought you'd know—"

Spencer hung up the phone, grabbed his coat and ran from the police department. He pulled out of the parking lot, heading straight to Glenn Oaks Hospital.

The cop in him conjured up a variety of worst-case scenarios. Scenarios he didn't want to see or worry about. *Keep it together, Ryan.* He drew in a deep breath, reining in his emotions to analyze only the facts. And he didn't have many. All the way to the hospital, no matter how much his truck slid on the roads, his thoughts were all Tatum. Was she okay? Was she hurt? Scared?

Dammit.

The truck slipped all over the road, so he kicked it into four-wheel drive and gunned it. By the time he reached the hospital, his fingers ached from his death grip on the steering wheel. He parked his truck and ran into the emergency room, flashing his badge.

"I'm looking for Tatum Buchanan."

The nurse flipped through the list. "I'll take you." She stepped around the desk and led him past a row of curtained partitions. "She should be able to go home shortly. We just wanted to make sure her concussion isn't too severe."

That was good news. Not good enough to make him relax, but it was a start. "What happened?"

"Ice." The nurse smiled at him. "We've had half a dozen accidents tonight and all of them were cars sliding on the ice. She was lucky, could have been a lot worse. The guy who hit her is in surgery."

Spencer's gut clenched. She was okay. She was okay. It would all be okay when he saw her. When he knew she was safe. It was hard to breathe.

"Aileen," the nurse said. "The detective is here to see your patient, Tatum Buchanan."

"Spencer?" He heard Tatum's voice and turned. "What are you doing here?"

He stood frozen. She had a wide strip of gauze wound around her temple, her long blond curls pulled over her left shoulder. She looked fragile, small, in the bed. "Hey." He moved to her without thought, pressing a hand along her cheek. "Where else would I be?" he asked, sitting on the side of her bed. "I would have been here earlier if I'd known."

"I'm...I'm fine," she said.

"That bandage around your head says otherwise." His voice was garbled. She was okay. He reached for her, taking her hand in his. Feeling her, warm and soft, made it better. "Why were you on the roads?" he asked, willing himself to calm.

She swallowed, staring at their joined hands. "I...I needed something from the store."

He frowned. "In the middle of an ice storm?"

"I didn't know it was that bad." Her voice was brittle. "Lesson learned."

"I'm just glad you're okay." He drew in a deep breath, focused on being calm. She didn't know he'd been scared shitless. That the thought of something happening to her was… He swallowed, twining his fingers through hers. "You're okay."

She nodded, then winced.

He winced too, squeezing her hand in his.

"You didn't need to come," she murmured, softly. "How did you even know I was here?"

He needed to come. He had to come. He had no choice. And there was no way he was leaving. "Cop, remember. I've got connections."

"Well, I'm fine. And you're supposed to be working." She tried to pull her hand from his, but he held tight. "Not babysitting."

He held on to her hand, biting back all the words he wanted to say. But now wasn't the time. She was in a hospital bed, for crying out loud. Not the best time to lay his heart on the line. It might be wrong to ask her to love him, but he had no choice. He loved her. He knew he always would.

"Miss Buchanan, once we get the doctor to sign off on your paperwork, you're cleared to go." The nurse smiled. "You shouldn't be driving—"

"I'm pretty sure my car's totaled," Tatum teased, laughing softly.

He closed his eyes. He'd seen too many accidents and fatalities on nights like this. She was safe. And he'd be damned if he didn't make sure she stayed that way. Seeing her here, wide-eyed and fragile, kicked his protective side into overdrive and his heart pumping. He cleared his throat and stood. "I'll take her home."

"Spencer—"

"I'm taking you home." He couldn't look at her, afraid she'd see just how close he was to breaking down. Whether it was his right or not, he needed to be with her.

13

TATUM STRETCHED, FEELING all sorts of aches and pains. She rolled onto her side, wincing at the jolt of pain that ran along her right side. She lifted the blankets high enough to assess her body. It wasn't pretty. Her thigh was covered in angry bruises, so was her hip, shoulder and upper arm. She groaned, going limp against the sheets.

Everything ached.

"That's gotta hurt," Spencer said, standing in the doorway.

"It does." She nodded, dropping the blankets back into place.

"I brought you something." He sat on the edge of the bed, offering her some pain pills and a glass of water.

"Best present ever." She sat up and took the pills, aware that his eyes were fixed on her bruises. "I know it looks bad."

He winced, shaking his head. "Can't help thinking you had a guardian angel last night. I saw your car."

She wanted to reach for him. She loved the concern that creased his face. And hated herself for it.

She'd lied to him last night. And she would keep lying

to him. He didn't need to know she was coming to him. Or that she loved him. Or that the way she felt, how overwhelming it was, scared her. She didn't want to be scared. She didn't want to hurt. Seeing his face in the hospital room—tender, almost…loving—cut her deep.

She couldn't get lost in him, not again. She closed her eyes. Neither of them needed to get hurt again.

He took her hand. "Hungry?"

She shook her head, pulling her hand from his.

He sat there, but she didn't look at him. She couldn't. She tucked her hands under the blanket.

"You need to eat something. Those meds are strong." He paused. "People have been bringing food and drinks by all morning."

People he'd been there to greet.

"At least let me make you some toast?" His voice was low, gruff.

She nodded, wincing at the tug of her stitches and bruising.

"Easy." He reached for her, but let his hand drop.

She lay back, staring at the ceiling overhead. Her heart hurt. She hurt.

It was almost Christmas Eve. Their deal was over. Done. She could fly to California without making a big deal out of it. That was what she wanted, what she needed, to stay in control. For this to be over. No complications, expectations or declarations had been made. No permanent damage had been done. Now was the best time to let him go.

"Lucy was here at the crack of dawn. She went to get your antibiotics," he called out. "Mom made some tea." He reappeared, balancing a plate on a brightly wrapped Christmas present. "You got me a Christmas present?"

She sat up, remembering the sexy lingerie she'd bought

for a final fling. She'd imagined seducing him slowly, under the Christmas tree, a fire roaring in the background. But now the thought of sex on the floor in front of the fire made her body protest. And her chest ache.

He sat on the edge of the bed, handing her toast with a smile. "I thought we'd already decided our twelve days was gift enough."

"I can take it back," she offered, eager to return the lingerie and scarves in the box.

"You can't take it back," he said, excitement edging his voice. "Not if it's what I think it is."

"You know what it is?" Disappointment gripped her. Okay, so sexy lingerie wasn't the most original idea, but she'd felt empowered buying it.

He ran his fingers through her hair, tilting her head back so she had no choice but to look at him. "I think so. And, no, I don't think you'll be up for that, either."

She met his gaze then, surprised. "You really think naughty lingerie is going to spice things up that much?"

He was quiet, his brows rising.

"Spencer?"

"Lingerie?" he asked.

"What did you think it was?" she asked, looking up at him. Did she really want to know?

He shook his head, a huge grin on his face.

Yes, she did. "Come on," she encouraged.

"I was *way* off base."

She sat up, wincing at the pull and throb of her bruises.

He frowned. "You need to take it easy."

She scowled at him. "You need to tell me what you thought I'd bought you for Christmas."

He shook his head. "No. I don't."

"It can't be that bad," she argued, frustration and curiosity warring.

"It's *not* bad." He ran a hand over his face.

She was beyond curious. "Can you give me a hint?"

"It required batteries," he said, watching her expression.

She shook her head. "Batteries?"

He ran a hand over his face again. "That first night, we talked about spicing things up."

She stared at him. Spicing things up? If things were any spicier, she might explode. But then understanding dawned on her. "A vibrator? You thought I bought us a vibrator?" If anything, he'd demonstrated that a vibrator wasn't an essential tool for sexual satisfaction. And yet the flare of desire that rolled over her told her it might be a hell of a lot of fun.

"I told you, whatever you want, Tatum." He stared at her, the corner of his mouth lifting into a grin.

Whatever she wanted... Sex with Spencer. Sex with Spencer and a vibrator.

Spencer.

Her eyes stung again. *Dammit.* No. That was over. He just didn't know it yet.

"All you have to do is tell me." The rasp of his voice made her toes curl. "I...I'd pretty much do anything for you, you know."

Her throat was tight and dry, her lungs empty. It was hard to breathe. Harder to say, "It's almost Christmas Eve."

His grin faded as he reached up. His fingers traced her hairline, captured a long curl and wrapped it around his fingers. "Let's renegotiate the terms."

Was he only referring to sex? Or something more?

She didn't want to know. She'd come to terms with the past, almost. But, if he did want something more... She couldn't. No matter how tempted she might be.

This was Spencer. No one else came close. No one else had this sort of power over her. Which was the very reason this needed to end. Whether or not this connection was normal, it was dangerously powerful.

"I don't think so." She nibbled her toast.

"Why?" He let go of her curl.

She forced a smile. "Because it was good. No, great. Exactly what I needed. No strings. No complications. Just sensation. Thank you for showing me how good intimacy can be."

His face was rigid, the tightening of his jaw making the beat of her heart falter.

She hadn't expected him to reach up, to stroke his fingers along her cheek, to run his thumb along her lower lip. "Tatum, maybe I want strings—"

"No, Spencer. I can't." She turned her head, severing the contact. "I'm flattered but... Thank you for the toast."

"She up?" Lucy's voice echoed. "Just tell me you're not banging an injured woman?"

He stood, tucking the Christmas present under his arm. She stared at the toast, focused on chewing.

"I'll go, since Lucy's here." He walked out, leaving her door cracked open, preventing her from falling completely apart.

"MERRY CHRISTMAS." CADY WAS all smiles as she and Patton hung their coats in his mother's hall closet.

"You too," Spencer said, returning her hug and shaking his brother's hand.

"Patton showed me pictures of Tatum's car. Holy crap, she was lucky." Cady squeezed his arm. "She here?"

"She's in the kitchen with Mom." Spencer nodded, still numb from Tatum's casual brush-off. It was taking everything he had to be civil. When all he wanted to do was yell or punch something. Considering his bruises might be gone in time for wedding pictures, adding new ones wouldn't go over well.

Patton waited until Cady left before asking, "What happened?"

"Besides her wreck?" Spencer growled. He still hadn't recovered from that. And now… "Shook me up—I'm not gonna lie to you."

"And?" Patton asked, leveling him with his I-know-something's-going-on look. "Don't try to bullshit me."

He swallowed, his gaze bouncing around the room as he murmured, "She ended it." Saying it out loud made it worse.

Patton's hand rested on his shoulder. "I'm sorry, Spence."

"Can't blame her." He hesitated, knowing he was exposing more to his brother than he wanted. "Guess some things are too hard to recover from."

Patton looked at him, not saying a word. His expression was hard, unreadable. "You're not gonna give up?" Patton asked.

"I can't make her love me."

Patton sighed. "She's the one. She's always been the one."

"Not disagreeing with you." Spencer drew in a deep breath, trying to ease the tension as he added, "But thanks for the pep talk."

"That's what big brothers are for." Patton winked and headed toward the kitchen.

But Spencer didn't follow. He glanced at the clock. Eight o'clock. Christmas Eve. He should have four more hours to touch her whenever he wanted to. And, dammit, now that he knew she was saying goodbye, he wanted those four hours now more than ever.

Dinner was over, he'd made his way around the room and offered suitably affectionate holiday sentiments. And Tatum was in the kitchen, spending time with his family, instead of in his bed. As far as she was concerned, their time was up. While he couldn't keep his eyes off the damn clock.

He should leave. Not that he was looking forward to a night on the lumpy couch in the garage, but staying here was too much like torture. He finished off the beer in his hand and—fool that he was—headed into the kitchen.

Tatum sat at the table, patched and bruised, and poring over a family album. He loved the smile on her face, the easy laughter that filled the room when Cady turned the album page. That was all he wanted, right there. For her to be happy. Even better if he was the one who made her happy.

Maybe Patton was right. Maybe he had to fight harder—show her how much he loved her. How good they would be, outside of the bedroom and in. She had to give him a chance. The thought of losing her altogether made him hurt.

"Spencer, you were an adorable baby." Lucy grinned his way.

Tatum's gaze met his. Even with the bruising on her temple, she was the most beautiful thing he'd ever seen.

"Look at all those rolls," Cady added, tapping the picture.

"He's fat," Patton said, laughing. "Not chubby, but *fat* fat."

"Oh, hush," their mother said. "I'll find your baby book next and we'll see who wins pudgiest baby."

"Please," Cady agreed.

"Is this some sort of new holiday tradition I didn't know about?" Spencer asked. "Public humiliation?"

"There's no shame in you being an adorable baby, Spencer." His mother sighed. "You're so tense. I think you've gotten worse than Patton these days."

Everyone in the kitchen looked at him then. His brothers, his sisters-in-law and Tatum. She looked sad.

"He just needs some Christmas cheer." Lucy shoved a cup of eggnog into his hand. "Eat, drink, be merry," she said.

Conversation drifted back to him and his brother's childhood. Lucy patted a chair at the table, conveniently located beside Tatum, and he sat. He leaned her way, his hand itching to take hers. Instead, he studied her profile, the ease of her smile and the curve of her cheek.

She caught him looking. "What's wrong?" she asked him, softly.

He shook his head.

She frowned. "What is it?"

"It's almost midnight," he said, staring at her.

She swallowed, realization widening her green green eyes. "Oh…"

He could kiss her. He could tell her he loved her. But all he managed was "I…I want my time. Even if I have to take a rain check."

"A rain check?" she repeated, her cheeks turning a rosy hue.

He stopped breathing. More time with her. "A deal is a deal."

It was then that he realized the kitchen was silent.

"A rain check for what?" Cady asked.

"Did you two have plans tonight?" his mother asked, clearly delighted.

The silence stretched until it grew painful.

"We were going to watch *Elf*," Tatum said.

"I love that movie," Lucy gushed.

"Me too," Cady said, glancing back and forth between him and Tatum.

"Is this an exclusive viewing?" Patton asked, amused.

Spencer wanted to say yes. He wanted to tell his brother to go screw himself and the rest of his family to mind their own business.

"Of course not," Tatum said. "You're all welcome."

Spencer's heart sank. No matter how his hands ached to touch her, her answer was still no.

14

TATUM FINISHED CLEANING up the cups of cocoa, empty bowls of popcorn, half-eaten cookies and candy-cane wrappers. Lucy busied herself straightening the pillows and putting the television cabinet back to rights. And Spencer was asleep in the recliner in front of the fire. He'd dosed off halfway through the movie and had been snoring softly ever since. Every time she brushed past him, she hesitated.

"You ready for tomorrow?" Lucy asked.

Tomorrow. California. Leaving. She hoped, with time and distance, she could finally let go of Spencer. She couldn't exactly start over if she was holding on to the past. "Not quite."

"What time is your flight?" Lucy asked.

"Seven thirty," Tatum answered.

"On Christmas Day?" Lucy frowned. "You could have waited."

"I didn't know how depressing this year would be," Tatum admitted, sitting at the kitchen table.

"Not as bad as you thought it would be?" Lucy asked.

Tatum shook her head, smiling. Until now, it'd been great.

"Do you need a ride to the airport?" Lucy asked.

"No," Spencer said from the kitchen doorway, bleary-eyed and yawning. "I'm taking her."

"Well, hello, sleeping beauty," Lucy said. "Did we wake you with all of our cleaning?"

He smiled. "It's done. Looks like I woke up just in time."

Tatum couldn't hold back her answering smile. She didn't want tonight to be awkward. It was Christmas Eve, after all.

"Where's everyone else?" he asked.

"The movie ended about an hour ago," Tatum offered. "Zach and Patton were breaking down the extra tables and chairs at your mom's place."

"You slept through all that work too," Lucy said.

"My evil plan worked," Spencer said, turning the full force of his blue eyes on Tatum.

Tatum's heart thudded.

"Guess I'll be heading out," Lucy said, hugging Tatum. "Merry Christmas. I'll see you in Colorado for the wedding?"

Tatum nodded. "Can't wait. Thank you," she said, hugging Lucy.

She closed the door and turned to find Spencer leaning against the door frame.

"You don't have to stay up," she said. "I know how tired you are. Go to bed."

His eyes widened. "I will." He pushed off the wall. "How are you holding up?"

"I'm fine." She was tired and achy but she still needed to pack.

"Can I help?" he asked, following her as she flipped off all the lights.

She shook her head. "No. I just want to sit for a minute." She sat on the couch, staring into the fire.

He sat on the couch arm, not saying anything.

"I've got a taxi coming in the morning, Spencer."

"I'll take you." His voice rolled over her, warm and sure.

"No. Thank you." She scowled at him, laying her head back on the couch cushions.

He sat beside her, his proximity having an immediate effect on her. So did the concern in his voice as he asked, "Your head hurting?"

"You don't need to take care of me," she said. She felt good. Good enough to want him. Now. Badly.

"Why is me taking care of you a bad thing?" He frowned.

She frowned back. "Because…because I'm not your responsibility."

He frowned at her, then said, "Friends take care of each other."

She stared at him. *Friends?* That was all she was to him. Which was exactly what she'd wanted. So why the hell did it upset her to hear him say it out loud? *What is wrong with me?*

"If it was Lucy, would there be a problem?" he asked.

"No," she said. "But I'm not sleeping with Lucy."

"And you're not sleeping with me anymore." He smiled at her, but there was something off about that smile. He glanced at the mantel, his smile fading.

Her gaze followed. Almost midnight. Heat coiled in the pit of her stomach, setting an unexpected shiver along her spine.

He saw it. The clenching of his jaw, the slight flare of his nostrils… He moved from the end of the couch to kneel on the floor at her feet. But when he reached for her, she couldn't take it. She wanted his touch, craved the comfort and pleasure he'd give her. "Don't, please." Her voice wavered.

His jaw locked, clenched so rigidly she feared he'd crack a tooth.

She pressed a hand to her head, the dull ache turning into a more pronounced throb.

His expression shifted again, remote and distant. "You should rest."

"You should stop telling me what to do," she snapped, pushing off the couch to stand.

He frowned, rising to stand inches from her. "Why are you so pissed off? I'm playing by your rules. Rules you won't let me forget. Rules I would break if you'd let me."

"Spencer—" If he didn't leave soon, she was going to fall apart. "This was a mistake. I don't know what I was thinking… You and I—" She saw his eyes close, saw his hands fist at his sides. "I'm sorry." *I'm sorry I'm too scared to love you.* "I…I don't know where we go from here. If we *can* be friends. I'm pretty sure life would be easier for both of us if we weren't."

"I can't lose you again," he said, his tone flat, hard.

"You can't lose something you never had, Spencer. I can't do this again. Not with you. Let it go, please," she said, walking to her bedroom door.

"Dammit, Tatum, don't be like this—"

"Be like what?" she asked. "You're the one who keeps pushing this. I don't need your help. I don't want it." The lie rolled off her tongue, leaving a bitter taste of self-loathing. But she hesitated, unable to resist looking at him. "I'm sorry." *For so much.* He stood there, beautiful and tense, staring at her with searching eyes. "Good night, Spencer." She closed her bedroom door and her control broke.

His whispered "Merry Christmas, Tatum" was full of such anguish she almost opened the door. Almost. Instead, she slid down the wall, wrapped her arms around her knees and sobbed until the pain in her head rivaled the crushing pain in her heart.

SPENCER STOOD IN his black suit, wishing this day was over. The last five days had been hell. Attending the graveside service of Clint Taggart was the last straw.

Spencer watched Taggart's wife, the tears rolling down her cheeks as she clasped the hand of her young daughter. Taggart's other children were clustered around their mom, each looking lost and heartbroken. He was thankful his mother had lived a long life with his father before he passed. And that he'd grown up with a man in the house—as unyielding as he'd been.

"Not the way I want to go out," Patton said as they left the services for the airport. "But I'm sure it's a relief to know his death was an accident."

Clint's car had been found in a ditch four hundred miles north of Greyson, off some county road. After losing his job, he'd headed to a buddy's house to regroup. When he'd decided to come home, the weather intervened and sent him sliding off a bridge and into a ravine. He'd been dead for days.

"Doesn't make it any easier on his wife and kids."

"You don't think so?" Patton argued. "I think it'd be a hell of a lot easier. Clint may not have been the best cop on the force, but he wasn't doing something illegal. He wasn't hunted down by the bad guy. He had an accident. A tragic accident—but an accident."

Spencer didn't say anything.

Patton's phone rang, so he put it on speaker. "Yep."

"Patton, is Spencer there?" It was their mother.

"I'm here," Spencer answered.

"I'm trying to confirm rooms. Is Tatum still coming to the wedding?" she asked.

"I have no idea," Spencer answered honestly. He'd tried to think of Tatum as little as possible over the last few days. He ached for her, missed her. He'd picked up the phone a dozen times but never hit Send.

"You talked to her?" his mother asked.

"No," he snapped.

There was a long silence.

"Spencer Lee Ryan." His mother didn't tolerate disrespect. "You don't need to use that tone with me, young man. If you and Tatum are having trouble, that's your business. But I need to know—"

"Mom, can you give Lucy a call?" Patton intervened. "She'll know."

"Yes, yes, I'll do that. You two have a safe flight. We'll see you soon." And the line went dead.

"Promise me that whatever is going on between the two of you won't affect the wedding," Patton said.

His brother might be a sullen son of a bitch, but Spencer was happy for him. He'd be on his best behavior for the wedding. Spencer smiled. "Yes, sir."

It wouldn't be easy. Seeing Tatum would hurt. But not seeing her was worse. His heart felt like it was squeezed by a vise every second of every day for the last five days. It helped to know he would eventually recover, even if it felt like his world was coming apart.

Patton wasn't big on small talk, so Spencer didn't bother filling the silence. He stared at the same magazine pages for ten minutes, indulging in various reunion scenarios with Tatum. Reality would likely be cool civility, and that would be a stretch for him. It was too much to hope for more than that.

He dozed for the length of the flight and woke up with a crick in his neck. His mood continued to nose-dive when his luggage was nowhere to be found. And the rental car they'd requested wasn't ready. He paced the airport while Patton stayed busy—talking to Cady on the phone.

When they finally reached the hotel, he wanted a drink and, possibly, a nap.

His mother greeted him with a "Stop frowning" and a quick hug.

"Good to see you two," Zach said. "A little too much estrogen around here. Please tell me my big brothers have something big lined up for tonight?"

"You mean the bachelor-party thing?" Spencer asked, perking up.

Zach nodded.

Patton shook his head. "No. We're having rehearsal in an hour and dinner after that."

Zach and Spencer exchanged frowns.

"Buzz kill," Zach said, laughing.

Spencer's phone rang. It was the airline. They'd found his bag but wouldn't be able to deliver until the next afternoon.

"Spencer?" his mother asked.

"Airline found my bag," he said.

"Good. Can you pick up Tatum? Lucy said she's having a hard time getting a car." His mother waited, her blue eyes steady upon him.

Maybe picking up Tatum, alone, would give them a chance to deal with anything lingering—so nothing sullied the mood for Patton and Cady's big day.

He nodded. But after he'd hung up the phone and was driving toward the airport, he knew he had to be strong. He'd missed her, yes. He wanted her. He loved her. But Tatum had made it clear they were done and his heart was too shredded for more rejection.

15

TATUM SMOOTHED HER hands over her hair and straightened the tie on her sweater. Her skintight black pencil skirt, clinging cream wrap-sweater and tall black boots hadn't been the most practical traveling attire, but it had definitely drawn a lot of attention her way. Hopefully it would have the same effect on Spencer. He'd been right—they needed to talk. And even though she'd shut him down, she hoped he'd give her another chance. Being vulnerable was something she avoided at all costs. And she was nervous as hell.

The last five days had been good for her.

Gretchen had been a truly generous host, showing her the sights of San Diego, the coastal beauty and the friendly people. There'd been a lot of laughing, a lot of drinking, and too many late nights talking about what they wanted out of life.

Tatum hadn't wanted to bring up Spencer. But Gretchen had asked.

"Come on, I've been dying to know. This is the guy you compared everyone to? Your true love." She'd been teasing, but her words had struck a chord.

Spencer had always been her measuring stick. Even when he wasn't part of her life, he'd been there.

He *was* the only man she'd loved with all of her. Poor Brent never stood a chance. Even after the wedding, her defenses had stayed up.

With Spencer, her defenses crumbled. It was terrifying. And wonderful.

And the more she thought about him, the more she missed him, the more she realized she was a complete idiot. She knew why he'd told her the truth about their past. He loved her. He still loved her. Her whole I'm-in-control stance was a joke. She wasn't in control. Her fear was.

And being afraid of Spencer, of loving him, was the last thing she wanted.

Now she stood, eager and terrified, to see him. It had only been five days. But in those five days she'd gone from holding him at arm's length to holding him in her heart. She paced, bought a bottle of water at one of the news shops and was opening it when he walked in.

Keep it together.

His blue eyes found her immediately, the pull between them instantaneous. But she stood her ground and made him come to her. She didn't miss his head-to-toe inspection, or the fact that his jaw clenched so tight his teeth were in danger.

"Hi," he said, his voice raspy and low.

"Hi."

"You look…" He swallowed. "You look good. How's the head?"

She moved closer, using the electricity between them. She knew he wanted her. It seemed like the right place to start. She turned her head, leaning closer and lifting her hair to show him the scar. "Stitches are out. I'm still a little tender, though." Their proximity wasn't just affecting *him*. He smelled so good, too good. "And I have a patchwork of rainbow-colored bruises along my side." She lifted the front wrap of her sweater, exposing the plane of her stomach, her belly button and the remains of her yellow-green bruise.

His eyes lingered on her stomach. He swallowed, closing his eyes and drawing in a deep breath. He shoved his hands into his pockets and muttered, "I need to get my luggage. Then we can go."

"You look tired," she said. It was true. Not just tired. Worn-out. There were bags under his eyes. And his eyes looked…haunted. "Long week?"

His gaze searched hers. "Yes."

She held his gaze, unflinching. But when his attention wandered to her mouth she had to turn away. She wanted him to kiss her, oh so badly. But not yet. "Let's go get your bag."

She reached for the handle of her suitcase at the same time he did. Their fingers brushed, the stroke of skin on skin making her stomach tighten and her lungs empty. She'd missed him. This time, she leaned into him to draw his scent deep into her lungs. And when his hand wrapped around hers, tugging her into his arms, she melted. She could turn into him, press her lips to his neck… Instead, she pulled out of his hold and stepped back.

He stood there, staring down at her, his hand gripping her suitcase handle.

"Ready?" she asked, hoping she sounded unaffected. Because inside, she was on fire.

He nodded and set off toward the airline customer service desk.

While he spoke to the agent, she knocked her bag over,

spilling the contents onto the floor. So much for smooth. But as she bent to collect them she remembered he was fond of her ass. She straightened slowly, appreciating his sudden hiss of breath.

"Got it," he bit out.

She straightened, knowing she was teasing him but unable to stop. He couldn't seem to move. The plum lacy strap of her bra peeking from the deep V of her sweater had him mesmerized.

"Spencer?" she asked, laying one hand on his chest.

He glanced at her hand. But before he could cover it with his own she was moving toward the doors.

"Where are you parked?" she asked, glancing back over her shoulder.

He was staring at her rear—good. He frowned, tore his gaze away and pulled both suitcases behind him. The walk to the car was tricky. Her heels were tall and there was ice on the ground. Not to mention it was cold. But a padded coat wouldn't help with the whole remind-him-what-he's-getting part of her plan.

She climbed into the truck, the hem of her skirt riding up just enough to reveal she was wearing stockings and a garter belt. A garter belt that matched the bra she was wearing. Yes, she was playing dirty. And it was way outside her comfort zone but she could only hope it would work.

He started the truck, but they didn't move. From the corner of her eye, she saw the way he was looking at her thigh. And her stomach clenched, willing him to reach for her. She ran her hands over her skirt, smoothing the fabric over the slight glimpse of plum silk, and buckled her seat belt.

Awareness coursed through her. This wasn't how it was supposed to happen. He was the one who needed to be overcome with desire, not her. Instead, she was throbbing, wanting his hands on her, his lips… She cleared her throat. Cool, calm, collected.

Five minutes later, the car still wasn't moving. He was staring straight ahead, every muscle taut. Maybe she wasn't the only one fighting this crazy hunger.

"Is everything okay?" she asked.

He nodded, not looking at her, and put the truck in gear. They set off, navigating their way out of the airport and onto the highway. The silence grew unbearable.

"How are the wedding preparations going?" she asked.

He shrugged.

"When did you fly out?" she tried again.

"This morning," he answered. "With Patton. We had a funeral to go to."

She looked at him, surprised. "I'm so sorry, Spencer. Was it someone you were close to?"

"We worked together." His answer was curt.

"Was it on the job?"

He shook his head. "No. Car accident."

"I'm sorry for your loss." She wanted to touch him then, to offer some sort of comfort.

He looked at her, eyes blazing. "How was California?"

She swallowed. "It was wonderful."

His jaw ticked. "Have a good time?"

"A great time." She had. When she wasn't missing him. "I met some nice people. Gretchen has a brother who's a fireman, so he and some friends took us out one night. They were pretty hilarious." All of which was true. Gretchen's brother was a happily married father of two, but Spencer didn't need to know that.

"A fireman?" he repeated.

She nodded, wondering what he was thinking. "I tried a few new things too."

"Like?" he barked.

"Oh… Have you ever had Thai food?" she asked.

He shook his head.

"It's hot," she said, laughing. "My eyes were watering and my tongue felt paralyzed. Even the next morning."

"What else?" he asked.

"Tequila shots," she said. "They're yummy. But they make me a little crazy."

He looked at her then. "Crazy?"

"Zip lining." She waved her hand at him. "I had fun."

"Good." But his tone implied he wasn't pleased.

"Are there any plans for tonight? I'd love a nap. Maybe even a soak in a hot tub," she added, enjoying his reactions far more than she'd expected.

"Rehearsal, rehearsal dinner, that's it," he ground out.

"No bachelor party?" She paused. "Or bachelorette party?"

He shook his head as they pulled into the hotel driveway. She waited for the valet to open the door and climbed out, offering a smile. Spencer was immediately at her side, his hand big and warm on her back, steering her inside before she'd had a chance to inspect her surroundings. Not that she cared. Right now the only thing she was aware of was Spencer. And if she didn't put some space between them soon, she'd be throwing herself at him in no time.

Not yet.

"Key," he said, offering her the card key.

"Thank you." She took it. "Guess I'll go make myself presentable."

His eyes swept over her again.

She left him standing there and headed for the elevators. But when she climbed onto the elevator, he followed, pulling his suitcase behind him.

TATUM WAS IN serious danger. If the old man left them alone in the elevator, Spencer could not be held accountable for his actions. He'd never been this close to losing control. But seeing her in her skintight getup, knowing what she had on underneath, had his dick at attention and his brain malfunctioning.

When they arrived on floor seven, he brushed past her, eager to get to his room and take a cold shower. But she followed him down the hall until he reached his room. She went around him, to the door next to his.

"Looks like we're neighbors," she said, smiling his way.

He nodded stiffly, trying not to think about the fact that she'd be so close. His hands fumbled with his card key, dropping it.

She disappeared into her room.

"Dammit," he growled, picking up his key and resting his forehead on the hotel room door. She'd gone off to California and hung out with firemen? She'd tried new things? And come home wearing what she was wearing. He adjusted himself, his erection pressing against his already fitted pants.

He tried his key. It didn't work. He tried again. Still nothing. He punched the wall. "Dammit," he bit out.

He stared at her door.

He could go downstairs and have them fix it. Or he could call from her room…

He knocked on her door.

"Who is it?" she asked through the door.

"Spencer," he answered. He took a deep breath. *Stop*

being an asshole. Stop snapping and growling at everyone.

She opened the door. "What's up?"

"My key doesn't work." She was so beautiful, so soft. His hand itched to touch her, to stroke her cheek and slide through the length of her silky hair. "Can I call the front desk?"

"Sure," she said, stepping back.

He heard the sound of running water. A passing glance saw bubbles piling up in her bath. "Sorry," he murmured.

"About what?" she asked.

"Interrupting." His mind was assaulted with images of her naked. Her body flushed and wet... He swallowed, running a hand over his face.

She twisted her hair up, clipping it in place on the back of her head. "Are you sure you're okay?" she asked, her hands fiddling with the tie of her sweater. "You seem so...tense."

"I'm fine." He didn't sound fine. He sounded like he was going to explode. Probably because he *was* going to explode.

"You want to talk about it?" she asked. "It's what friends do. Talk."

His heart twisted. "So we can be friends?"

She shrugged. "I'd like to try. I've never seen you like this and I want to be here for you if I can. If you want me?"

He closed his eyes. "If I want you?" he muttered. "That's the problem, Tatum. That's the whole damn problem." He sounded harsh to his own ears.

"What?" she asked, startled.

"I want you." He moved forward. "I can't stop." His hands clasped her shoulders, pulling her against him. "So, no, I don't want to talk about it."

"Then what do you want?" she whispered.

"You." He bent, nuzzling her neck. "Dammit." She smelled like heaven. "Now."

She drew in an unsteady breath as his lips latched on to her neck. His hands slid through her hair, tugging her head back so he could taste her. His tongue slid between her lips, tearing a moan from her and racking him with a shudder.

He deepened the kiss, cradling the back of her head to explore the recesses of her mouth and leave them both reeling.

Her hands twined in his hair, shattering whatever remained of his self-control. He gripped her hips, lifting her up as he drove her back against the wall. He dropped to his knees, sliding the tie of her sweater free and pulling it down to her wrists—pinning them at her sides. With mounting impatience, he tugged her skirt until it was around her hips. He paused long enough to take in the view.

"You're so damn beautiful," he ground out, running his fingers across the plane of her stomach. She was gasping, her eyes pressed closed, her hands tightly fisted at her sides. He ran one finger along the garter, pressed a kiss at the edge of her filmy panties and gripped her ankle. He worked his way up her silk-clad calf, nuzzling the soft skin behind her knee until she was shuddering. He pressed her back, keeping her in place, while forcing her legs apart. His lips skimmed her heated flesh as his hand slid up the back of her leg. He lifted her leg, staring up at the raw need on her face. She needed release… and he would give it to her. When his hand cupped the curve of her ass, he nipped the velvet soft skin of her inner thigh.

"Spencer." Her voice broke, urgent.

He hooked her thigh over his shoulder. One hand gripped the soft curve of her ass, the other braced himself—holding her wrist against the wall.

Her panties were barely there, the frothy G-string hiding nothing. He nudged it aside with his nose and bent to his work. Her scent, the taste of her, overwhelmed his senses. She was ready, her skin contracting at the first stroke of his tongue. He kneaded the swell of her buttock, parting her for the slide of his fingers. He was relentless, his fingers deep, his lips and tongue working the tight nub at her core. On and on, he pushed her until she cried out, her hands slamming against the wall and her hips arched forward.

She slumped against the wall, spent and gasping.

He pushed off the wall, his breath powering from his lungs and blood on fire. His need for her was almost painful. But there was more. He knew he had no right to ask her to love him. But, right now, he had no choice. He loved her, he'd always loved her. It wasn't about wanting her body—it was about wanting her. He sucked in a deep breath, his heart pounding in his ears. "Tatum," he groaned. "I'm sorry. I… Damn, I…I hadn't planned on this happening."

The ragged sound of her breathing stopped. In that instant she went from soft and spent to wary. "No, don't apologize. You didn't do anything I didn't want."

He stared down at her, cupping her cheek. She still wanted him. That was something. "I missed you, Tatum."

She drew in a deep breath. "I had a lot of time to think while I was gone." She frowned. "You're right—we need to talk, I have a lot I want to say, but maybe now's not the right time." She shrugged away from him, her cheeks red.

"Why?" he argued, reaching for her. He needed to

touch her, to feel her, to know she was there. "Maybe there's no such thing as the right time. But there is right now." Panic pressed in on him. He knew what she was going to say. She was going to San Diego, she was going to leave him. Better to rip the damn Band-Aid off now. "Just say it."

"You have a hard-on. My skirt is around my waist." She sounded defeated as she pushed the clinging fabric back into place. "If we are going to talk, I need to know your words aren't coming from here." She grabbed his erection, making him jolt. "I'd like to know that your words are coming from here." She pressed her hand to his heart, then his head.

"Tatum, say it," he all but growled.

She looked so...nervous that his heart stopped. "I love you," she whispered. "I love you, Spencer."

Her phone was ringing. When it had started, he didn't know. And, at the moment, he didn't care. But the ringing sent Tatum into a tailspin, smoothing her tangled hair into place and holding her sweater closed.

He frowned, reaching for her, trying to process what he'd heard. She loved him? She loved him, and he was staring at her like an idiot.

She answered her phone. "Hey, Lucy."

He wasn't prepared for the anxious look in her eyes. Or the uncertainty on her face. "He's here," she said. "His key doesn't work." She paused. "I'll send him down."

Did she seriously doubt how he felt? Because he'd be happy to fix that—now.

He waited as she hung up the phone.

"Your mother needs you now," she said, brushing past him into her bathroom. "Don't forget to have your key fixed."

"Tatum—"

"Tonight is about Patton and Cady," she murmured.

"You can't seriously expect me to leave now?" he asked, putting his hand on the bathroom door. And ignoring the persistent ring of his phone.

She grinned. "I'd like to stay on your family's good side. And my bath is getting cold."

She shut the bathroom door in his face. He stood there, staring at the door. He pressed a hand against the door. "I can wash your back," he offered.

"Go, Spencer," she called back, laughing. "We can talk after. When I'm dressed and you're thinking straight."

He was reeling. She loved him. The ache that filled his chest didn't compare with the ache of his body. He wanted Tatum, there was no denying that—to the point of addiction. But he loved her beyond that.

He knew his life was risky. But life was risky. He'd rather face any adversity with her at his side than without her.

And he wanted her to know that—wanted everyone to know that.

His phone rang, making him cuss under his breath. He glanced at the screen before tucking it into his pocket. Once the wedding was over, he'd make sure Tatum knew exactly how he felt. And how damn good their future was going to be—together.

16

TATUM WATCHED CADY and Patton move around the dance floor. It had been a gorgeous wedding. And, considering how firmly Patton insisted he wasn't a fan of weddings, he seemed to be enjoying himself. Or maybe he was just happy to be married.

"You look gorgeous," Lucy said, sitting beside her.

"So do you." It was true. The Ryans were a good-looking family.

"Dean's been checking you out," Celeste added.

"Dean's checking all the single ladies out," Tatum argued.

"Anyway, Spencer wins. He's almost walked into a wall twice. I'd say you two might finally be making progress?" Lucy asked.

Finally. He loved her—even if he hadn't said as much yet. She glanced at the dance floor. Spencer was dancing with his mother. He was laughing, his head thrown back—looking so gorgeous her heart hurt. They made their way to the front of the room, to join Cady and Patton.

"Looks like speech time," Celeste said, reaching for her champagne.

Cady went first. She was sassy and funny, making everyone laugh. But when she hugged her new husband, the tenderness on her face said it all.

"Cady showed me what it meant to live. Now all I want is to live every day with her." Patton's speech was short, but—from him—was truly touching.

Then Spencer took the microphone. "If my father were here, he'd say this toast. But, as he's not, I will. May you live as long as you want, and never want as long as you live. May the blessings of each day be the blessings you need most. May you have warm words on a cold evening, a full moon on a dark night. And the road downhill all the way to your door." Spencer paused. "My brothers are amazing men. Good sons, good husbands. They work hard, keep their word, are unwaveringly loyal, and when they fall in love—it's forever." He paused, his gaze finding and holding hers. He waited until everyone in the room knew he was looking at her before he continued, "I'd like to think I've learned from the best. Patton, Cady, congratulations."

Tatum stared at him, stunned. Her heart was tripping over itself.

When they fall in love—it's forever.

"Want to dance?" Dean asked, holding his hand out to her.

She was still processing Spencer's words as he led her onto the dance floor. He spun her into him, winking at her. She laughed, squealing when he dipped her.

"Is it a prerequisite for the Ryans to dance?" she asked, breathless when he spun her around.

"Yes. Aunt Imogene had a friend that owned a dance academy. She made us all take lessons, out of solidarity." Dean shook his head. "You look gorgeous."

"You don't look too bad yourself," she said, trying to keep up with him. While covertly searching for Spencer.

"He's behind you," Dean said.

Her heart stopped. "He is?"

"He's headed this way," Dean said, nodding. "Looks pretty pissed off to me."

"He does?"

"Not that he deserves you," Dean continued.

She smiled at him, pressing a kiss to his cheek. "You're a good guy, Dean."

He looked down at her. "Let's keep that our secret."

"Cutting in," Spencer said sharply.

She stared at him. "Is that a request?"

Spencer sighed, closing his eyes and taking a deep breath. "Yes. It is. May I cut in?"

"Watch it," Dean said. "She's all handsy."

She giggled, a mix of nerves—and hope.

Dean left, leaving them alone on the dance floor.

"Did you hear my speech?" he asked.

She nodded.

"What did you think?"

She brushed the hair from his forehead. "You love me?"

"Yes."

"I admit that makes me happy. Happier than I've ever been." She swallowed.

"I love you." He stopped dancing, cradling her face in his hands. "Always."

She sucked in a deep breath, feeling light and oh so blissful. She couldn't stop smiling.

He rested his forehead against hers. "Are you going to California? If you are, I need to get my résumé in order."

She laughed. "You'd go?"

He nodded, his expression stern. "I go where you go. I want what you want."

"You do?" Her fingers brushed through the hair at the nape of his neck. "And if all I want is you? And for you to love me."

"Done."

"No moving. Cady's already convinced half of Greyson I should handle their books."

"This is what you want?" His voice was low.

"As long as we have each other." She paused, the emotions she'd been fighting for so long clogging her throat. "I have exactly what I want."

He pulled her closer, swaying to the music. "I didn't know how much I'd missed you until you waved that poker at me on the front porch."

"I didn't wave it at you," she argued, laughing.

"Nothing has ever scared me like thinking I'd lost you again."

She stared up at him. "I'm sorry, Spencer. I promise, I'm not going anywhere."

"I'll hold you to it." He kissed her lips. "And you love me?"

"I love you," she said between kisses.

"Now, let's talk about that rain check." He ran his thumb along her lower lip.

"No more talking," she said, pulling his mouth to hers.

* * * * *

REQUEST YOUR FREE BOOKS!
2 FREE NOVELS PLUS 2 FREE GIFTS!

⊕ HARLEQUIN®

Blaze
red-hot reads!

YES! Please send me 2 FREE Harlequin® Blaze novels and my 2 FREE gifts (gifts are worth about $10). After receiving them, if I don't wish to receive any more books, I can return the shipping statement marked "cancel." If I don't cancel, I will receive 4 brand-new novels every month and be billed just $4.74 per book in the U.S. or $5.21 per book in Canada. That's a savings of at least 14% off the cover price. It's quite a bargain. Shipping and handling is just 50¢ per book in the U.S. and 75¢ per book in Canada.* I understand that accepting the 2 free books and gifts places me under no obligation to buy anything. I can always return a shipment and cancel at any time. Even if I never buy another book, the two free books and gifts are mine to keep forever.

150/350 HDN GH2D

Name	(PLEASE PRINT)	

Address		Apt. #

City	State/Prov.	Zip/Postal Code

Signature (if under 18, a parent or guardian must sign)

Mail to the **Reader Service:**
IN U.S.A.: P.O. Box 1867, Buffalo, NY 14240-1867
IN CANADA: P.O. Box 609, Fort Erie, Ontario L2A 5X3

Want to try two free books from another line?
Call 1-800-873-8635 or visit www.ReaderService.com.

* Terms and prices subject to change without notice. Prices do not include applicable taxes. Sales tax applicable in N.Y. Canadian residents will be charged applicable taxes. Offer not valid in Quebec. This offer is limited to one order per household. Not valid for current subscribers to Harlequin Blaze books. All orders subject to credit approval. Credit or debit balances in a customer's account(s) may be offset by any other outstanding balance owed by or to the customer. Please allow 4 to 6 weeks for delivery. Offer available while quantities last.

Your Privacy—The Reader Service is committed to protecting your privacy. Our Privacy Policy is available online at www.ReaderService.com or upon request from the Reader Service.

We make a portion of our mailing list available to reputable third parties that offer products we believe may interest you. If you prefer that we not exchange your name with third parties, or if you wish to clarify or modify your communication preferences, please visit us at www.ReaderService.com/consumerchoice or write to us at Reader Service Preference Service, P.O. Box 9062, Buffalo, NY 14240-9062. Include your complete name and address.

"You dumped me after one night and said you couldn't
date an inferior."

"I didn't say that. I said I was your superior and
therefore could not date you. You remember that part
about me being your boss?"

"Only for two more weeks."

"What are you going to do?"

"I got a new job. A better job."

"Better? Better than here?"

She almost rolled her eyes.

"Yes, Ian, believe it or not. I would also like to have
a job where I don't weld all day and then go home and
weld some more for my other life. You can't blame me
for that."

"I don't, no. You've stuck it out here longer than
anyone thought you would."

"I had to fight tooth and nail to earn the respect of
the crew. I'm a little tired of fighting to be treated like a
human being. You can't blame me for that, either."

So, yeah, she was thrilled about the new job.

But.

But…Ian.

It wasn't just that he was good in bed. He was. She remembered all too well that he was—passionate, intense, sensual, powerful, dominating, everything she wanted in a man. The first kiss had been electric. The second intoxicating. By the third she would have sold her soul to have him inside her before morning, but he didn't ask for her soul, only every inch of her body, which she'd given him for hours. When she'd gone to bed with him that night, she'd been half in love with him. By the time she left it the next morning, she was all the way in.

Then he'd dumped her.

Six months ago. She ought to be over it by now. She wanted to be over it the day it happened but her heart wasn't nearly as tough as her reputation. The worst part of it all? Ian had been right to dump her. They'd both lost their heads after a couple drinks had loosened their tongues enough to admit they were attracted to each other. But Ian had a company to run and there were rules—good ones—that prohibited the man who signed the paychecks from sleeping with the woman who wielded the torch.

Don't miss ONE HOT DECEMBER
by Tiffany Reisz, available December 2016 everywhere
Harlequin® Blaze® books and ebooks are sold.

www.Harlequin.com

Reading Has Its Rewards

Earn **FREE BOOKS!**

Register at **Harlequin My Rewards** and submit your Harlequin purchases from wherever you shop to earn points for free books and other exclusive rewards.

Plus submit your purchases from now till May 30th for a chance to win a $500 Visa Card*.

Visit **HarlequinMyRewards.com** today

MYR16R1

HARLEQUIN®

A *Romance* FOR EVERY MOOD™

JUST CAN'T GET ENOUGH?

Join our social communities
and talk to us online.

You will have access to the latest
news on upcoming titles and special
promotions, but most importantly,
you can talk to other fans about your
favorite Harlequin reads.

Harlequin.com/Community

Facebook.com/HarlequinBooks

Twitter.com/HarlequinBooks

Pinterest.com/HarlequinBooks